Miss Darcy's Beaux

ELIZA SHEARER

ISBN 10: 154650110X

ISBN 13: 9781546501107

Miss Darcy's Beaux

ELIZA SHEARER

For my very own Captain Wentworth

Chapter 1

The nervous steps up and down the main Pemberley staircase must have woken me up. When you've spent most of the twenty years of your life in a house, you know its every single sound and murmur, and the slightest nuance can raise you from your sleep. The staircase, in beautiful Italian marble, was a striking feature and a suitably grand adornment to the vestibule of one of the most coveted properties in England. It was also perilously slippery underfoot for those in a hurry. That wasn't so much of a problem for us, the family, as we were going about our business, but it was the main reason why the servants avoided it whenever possible, especially when they were on an urgent errand, and preferred to use the service stairways crisscrossing the building instead.

I opened my eyes but couldn't see a thing. No light was filtering into my room through the thick blue velvet curtains. I sighed, turned in my bed and tried to go back to sleep. Then I heard those footsteps again, now followed by hushed voices. Something was going on. A thought startled me. Elizabeth's baby! I quickly pulled back the covers, threw on my shawl and headed downstairs, holding a candle in my shaking hand.

I walked towards the flickering lights and human shadows at the other end of the corridor, where my brother and his wife had established their rooms. I heard the voice of Dr Robertson, the physician. He had only recently settled in Lambton, but he had quickly become a regular visitor at Pemberley, mainly due to my brother's faith in modern medicine. However, Elizabeth's attitude towards the new medic was not as enthusiastic, and I had my reasons to suspect why.

The main door to their apartment was ajar. Right outside was an old crone I recognised immediately as Mrs Brown. She was a local midwife with a reputation for being very competent and knowledgeable, but a most disconcerting local accent and the unfortunate habit of always sniffling and mumbling to herself. I had always fancied the woman to be some sort of a witch, but Elizabeth had taken a liking to her during her first pregnancy and requested she visit on a few occasions during this one. I remembered the look of shock on Mrs Reynolds, the old housekeeper, when my sister-in-law insisted on Mrs Brown waiting in the kitchen when she was about to give birth, should complications arise. Elizabeth seemed to have blind faith in the crone's abilities in the event of an emergency, and Dr Stuart, Dr

Robertson's predecessor, had been happy to indulge her.

Thankfully, the midwife's services weren't required when my first nephew Will was born. Dr Stuart himself had remarked on the ease of the birth. But this time things were different. For starters, Dr Robertson didn't approve of Elizabeth's continued pursuit of long country walks and exercise in the fresh air in her condition. It had taken a number of worrying and unpleasant incidents, each of them closely followed by a visit from Dr Robertson, to convince her to alter her energetic habits. My brother's support of the physician's orders had been paramount to ensure Elizabeth's reluctant acquiescence.

Eager for news, I accosted Mrs Brown, but she barely acknowledged my presence. She was mumbling something unintelligible, and her eyes were focused on what was taking place inside the rooms. I followed her gaze and saw Fitzwilliam, his back stiffer than usual and his head slightly tilted in what most people would say was impatience and even self-importance, but I quickly identified as helplessness. He was waiting in the small study adjacent to the main bedroom he shared with his wife, longingly glancing towards the closed door with the look of a dog awaiting his owner. I tiptoed towards him and hesitantly put a hand on his shoulder. He shook under my touch, then realised it was me.

"Georgiana, I hope you have not been disturbed".

"What's the matter, Brother?"

His eyes hadn't left the door.

"Mrs Darcy was feeling some discomfort, and Dr Robertson

has been called for. He is attending to her at the moment. It shouldn't be long now."

"Is that the reason why Mrs Brown is here?"

Fitzwilliam faintly nodded.

"Mrs Darcy made me promise that, should Dr Robertson come to see her, Mrs Brown would be called for as well."

The bedroom door opening interrupted him and we both turned to Dr Robertson, who was coming out of his patient's bedchamber. The physician's face was as grave as always, but there was no second-guessing him. One always had to wait for the very end of his speeches to find out the gravity of any situation. I suspect he enjoyed holding his audience in suspense at times like these.

The physician slowly placed his bag on a chair next to the door and took from his pocket a perfectly ironed white handkerchief, with which he proceeded to clean his spectacles with deliberation, as if the centre of the universe revolved around the hygiene of this particular item. My brother was impatient. He looked at Dr Robertson pointedly, as if to remind him that he was expected to provide news on the lady of the house, but to my surprise, the physician addressed me first.

"Miss Darcy, I see that the events we're presently dealing with have interrupted your sleep. Such an ungodly hour, but that is the nature of the matter we have in our hands."

I acknowledged him with a tilt of my head but didn't say anything. Dr Robertson then gave my brother a stern look.

"Mr Darcy, as I have explained in the past, Mrs Darcy has an enviably healthy constitution, but she is in a most delicate state. I realise the first time around everything went very well, and that no assistance was required over several months other than the little support that was provided by that... *woman*."

Dr Robertson shuddered slightly. I wondered if Mrs Brown, who was waiting just outside the room, could hear us. The physician put his spectacles back on. Behind the lenses, his eyes grew noticeably bigger, and made me think of the big and cumbersome flies that tended to congregate around the picnic basket fare during summer day trips. With the utmost gravity, the physician continued.

"On that occasion, Mrs Darcy was most fortunate. Not all ladies can say the same when it comes to their first confinement, and later ones don't necessarily become easier either. In fact, it is no surprise to me that this time around she is not feeling as energetic as in the past. It is just what's to be expected."

Not for the first time, I pondered whether Dr Robertson's fondness for leeching his patients, a practice he recommended most vehemently and that Elizabeth had recently undergone, had helped or hindered my sister-in-law's natural vigour. However, I didn't open my mouth. In spite of my misgivings, I wouldn't have dared to challenge the physician's knowledge, much less in front of my brother.

"Mrs Darcy apparently believes the old wives' tale that exercise is not to be shunned by expectant mothers. Nevertheless, as I have made clear to her on numerous occasions, although women from the lower classes do not cease to go about their business in their usual manner, the situation is very different for ladies of *her* position."

Here, Dr Robertson arched his eyebrows, and allowed the silence that followed to speak for him.

My brother swallowed hard, and I felt myself blush. It's not that I didn't like Elizabeth, or didn't think that she was the ideal wife for my brother. Quite the opposite, in fact: she was perfect in every way, the best sister-in-law I could have wished for. She was witty, amusing and affectionate, and had transformed Pemberley from an overly formal stately residence to a family home full of laughter, not least thanks to the presence of my cherubic nephew, Will. More intriguingly, since her appearance in our lives I had begun to see and love a different side to my brother, one he had always kept to himself until that point. Elizabeth was a wonderful mother to little Will, but she was an even better influence on Fitzwilliam, who so readily bore the full weight of all sorts of responsibilities, from the financial situation of the estate to the wellbeing of every single one of its residents and tenants, on his shoulders.

However, at times like these, in passing comments such as the one Dr Robertson had just made, we the Darcys were mercilessly reminded of the change my sister-in-law's alliance with our family had meant to her station. Elizabeth's marriage to my brother had required no small transformation in her habits, but no matter how successful her achievements as mistress of Pemberley, a role most young women would be ill-prepared to embody, no matter how careful their upbringing, with every one of her actions she faced the age-old prejudices of some of our friends and family, with my aunt, Lady Catherine de Bourgh, at the helm. Even some servants at the beginning of their married life had shown their displeasure at the new lady of the house, their disapproval swiftly nipped in the bud by my brother, who had chosen for them alternative placements in rarely visited family properties away from Pemberley.

Asserting herself as a Mrs Darcy worthy of the privilege was an eternal struggle that someone less capable than Elizabeth would not have found the strength and inclination to continue. However, my sister-in-law was always gracious about the stares, the suspicious looks, the schadenfreude comments that pretended concern for that which she had not yet mastered. She was so lovely, graceful and clever that most people forgot about their reservations surprisingly quickly upon meeting her in person. But some resistance always remained. And then, of course, there was her family.

The Bennets represented a far from desirable alliance for the heir of the Darcys of Derbyshire. On a rare occasion, a few days before his wedding, Fitzwilliam admitted as much to me. I caught him admiring the portrait of Mama that hung above the fireplace in the library, painted when he was a toddler. She looked radiant in a cream silk gown in the old fashion, her tiny waist cinched by a thick black belt and her elaborate powdered wig covered with a beautiful little hat secured with a muslin scarf. My brother confessed that, from the moment he had met the Bennets at a ball in Meryton, he had questioned the propriety of some family members. However, he had also been quick to recognise what a wonderful Mrs Darcy Elizabeth would make. As he said so, his dark eyes softened, and they rather reminded me of our old pointer Sarpedon's, the one I had begged Fitzwilliam not to put down because the thought broke my heart.

The fact was that my brother had made his choice with as much deliberation as a man in love can muster, and now he had to bear the consequences of his actions. Most of the time, fortune and privilege meant that he had the power to remove himself from any unpleasantness, but on occasion, he simply had to grin and bear it. His relationship with the Lambton physician fell squarely in this second category. I doubted Fitzwilliam was very fond of him, but my brother adored his wife, and was convinced that Dr Robertson's services were paramount to ensure a healthy and happy delivery of their second baby.

As if to break the silent spell cast by his words, the physician coughed and adjusted his lenses. My brother's gaze hadn't left him for a single second since he had stepped out of the room where Elizabeth was resting, and he surely knew it. Puffing up his chest with self-importance, Dr Robertson finally delivered his verdict.

"Mrs Darcy must go into confinement with immediate effect. I am afraid I cannot allow her to leave her room or her health may be severely affected."

Fitzwilliam's eyes widened. Dr Robertson raised his right hand with authority.

"I must insist, Mr Darcy. Absolute rest from now on. I will be back tomorrow morning for some bloodletting."

I heard a grunt coming from behind me. It would appear that Mrs Brown not only had witnessed the whole exchange, but also didn't quite agree with Dr Robertson's remedy. As was his custom, the physician ignored the old woman. He put his handkerchief back in his pocket and, after commending my brother be most pressing in convincing Elizabeth to follow his instructions, he left.

All of a sudden, Fitzwilliam looked fatigued.

"Doctor's orders, then. She won't be able to say no," he said, rubbing his forehead with his long fingers. In a soft voice he added, "Georgiana, it's very late. I will see you in the morning."

He opened the door to his bedroom and went back inside without making a noise. I headed towards the dark corridor, my candle now about to perish, and immediately bumped into someone who smelled of hay, sweat and sour milk. It was Mrs Brown. But the midwife didn't appear to take any notice of me. She was shaking her head, and this time I was able to make sense of her words.

"Poor lady, poor lady..."

Slipping through the shadows like a cat, with my heart filled with worry, I went back to my bedchamber.

Chapter 2

The following morning I breakfasted alone. I was informed that my brother had had to leave early after receiving an urgent notice from Mr Harvey, the estate keeper, and that Elizabeth was convalescing in her room. I was eager to see her, but it was still early. Looking out of the window I saw that the sun was out and the ground was dry, so I fetched my warmest shawl and stepped outside.

It was a bright, mild day in late February. The grounds at Pemberley had not looked as inviting in months. The winter frost was giving way to patches of green, and tiny buds were visible everywhere. I first thought of heading west towards the formal garden, but the pull of the morning sun was strong, and I headed eastwards, towards the majestic willows that grew by the stream, imposing in the barren landscape. Here and there, I could see timid dashes of colour. Where there had been snowdrops, there were primroses, their beautiful blooms opening as if they were as starved of sunlight as I was after a long winter confined in the house. The nests that had shown such industriousness in the summer and spring had been empty for months, but would soon have new occupiers.

The sun was getting stronger by the minute, and I realised I didn't have a parasol with me. I hadn't thought I would need one this early in the day. Mrs Younge's words resonated unwelcome in my thoughts. 'Your porcelain skin is your best asset, Miss Darcy, and you should make sure it remains so,' she used to say. She was extremely vigilant when it came to my complexion; unfortunately, she was much less concerned about my virtue. I blushed in spite of myself. The disgraceful event was safely in my past, at least.

My walk had led me to the pond where, as a little girl, Wickham had taken me on tadpole hunts. I remembered the long summers together, his playfulness, his attentiveness, the way he had of combing his hair back with his fingers. Wickham was fond of telling me stories. According to him, the tadpoles were an army of disguised soldiers, ready to defend Pemberley from a terrible dragon that hid behind the hills. He used to say that the minute the beast attacked us, Mr Tiddles the cat would become a white horse, and his trusty pocket knife would turn into a majestic sword, ready for action. As he said this, his arm would be up in the air, waving an invisible weapon, and his eyes would sparkle, eager for the fight.

I sighed. The stories came when my brother was in the study, learning the ropes of estate management. From an early age, my father had been eager to educate his son and heir in the affairs that in due course would become his responsibility, and my brother had applied himself to the task, his conscientiousness and sense of duty as much a part of him as his dark hair. But away from the house, things were different for Wickham and me. In those long afternoons, if the weather was good, we were allowed to play outside under the supervision of Nanny Fraser, the Pemberley nursemaid. Wickham would walk by her side, his charm oozing from his every pore. We'd reach the pond, the poor woman quite out of breath as she was getting into old age; after all, Nanny Fraser had cared for Mama and her brother and sister when they were little. Wickham, ever the gentleman, would then guide her towards a lonely bench in the perfect shady spot, overlooking the house, and say 'Nanny Fraser, won't you sit down? We've had a fair bit of exercise. I'll play with Georgiana right there. I'll look after her, don't you worry.' The old nursemaid would grumble a bit, saying that she just needed to get her breath back, and take a seat, insisting that she would be with us in a few minutes, but invariably she would be snoring after a short while.

As soon as Nanny Fraser was asleep, Wickham would take my hand and drag me to the pond. He taught me to put my hands in the water slowly, fingers gently touching, so as not to scare the tadpoles, then bring the edges of the palms swiftly together around an unsuspecting victim. Then came the hard bit, lifting the cage with the tadpole inside and enough water to keep it from wriggling out. Wickham often had to help me, and he would do so by covering my pudgy child hands with his.

As a young girl, I was in awe of Wickham, just as I was in awe of my brother for entirely different reasons. Where Wickham was stories and laughs, Fitzwilliam was concern and sternness. I loved my brother dearly, he was my picture of a perfect gentleman, but I was in love with Wickham even before I even knew what romance was. What followed, the folly of a fifteen-year-old girl eager to escape the sheltered world she had always lived in with the man she had always adored, came close to disgracing me forever. Thankfully, our idiotic plans had not come to fruition. Only just.

I felt the familiar jolt deep inside of me. It was weaker every time, but it was still there. I sighed again. The future that we might have shared, I could imagine, but I would never experience. And now Wickham was married to Lydia, Elizabeth's sister. I wondered, not for the first time, at the dissimilar natures of the five Bennet girls. Other than the fact that they were all pretty but for the middle one, Mary, who came across as positively plain next to the others, they all had very contrasting temperaments and sensibilities. How different that was from my brother and myself, so alike in disposition.

"Good morning dear Georgiana, may I join you?"

A friendly masculine voice jolted me back to reality. I looked up, a hand covering my eyes, as the sun was now much brighter that it had been since last autumn. Colonel Fitzwilliam was smiling at me. He was visiting Pemberley as was his habit this time of year, and his presence was welcome by us all. My brother appreciated having male company around, Elizabeth always enjoyed conversing with him, and for me, it was delightful to spend time with my older cousin and guardian, so well-travelled and full of stories. I smiled back and gestured him to sit down next to me on Nanny Fraser's bench.

We talked about the weather and the signs of the approaching spring, but the Colonel seemed melancholy, not quite his usual cheerful self, as if something was preoccupying him. He enquired after Mrs Darcy, who usually joined me in my morning walks, so I explained to him what had happened the previous night. In my retelling of the events I could feel myself speaking and breathing faster, and feeling more and more sombre, as if all of a sudden, the beautiful morning had lost all pleasure. Colonel Fitzwilliam listened attentively, without interrupting me once, until I had finished my explanations.

"I know how fond you are of Mrs Darcy, and indeed I think we all are," the Colonel said, looking grave. "Remaining bed-ridden will be a trial for her. I imagine her mother and sisters will be here soon."

That Mrs Bennet and her daughters may descend upon Pemberley simply hadn't occurred to me. All my fantasies to entertain Elizabeth during her convalescence by reading out loud Shakespeare's plays and Scott's novels were stamped upon by an army of satin-slippered feet. My face must have given away my disappointment because the Colonel immediately gestured towards a particularly beautiful bush nearby that was beginning to flower. He stood up and offered me his arm; he insisted that we should have a look at it, which we did, and we continued to walk towards the house, his company providing me with great solace. It wasn't until we were by the main entrance that he spoke again on the matter.

"Georgiana, your brother and I have been thinking for a while that you should spend some more time in society other than the one Pemberley and its surrounding area can offer, and now may be a good time. If Mrs Darcy's relatives come to visit, she will have many sources of constant comfort and company during her remaining confinement. Your temporary absence will be much more endurable than under normal circumstances, both for her and for Darcy."

Leave Pemberley precisely at that moment! I was going to voice my objection, but the Colonel gently patted my sleeve.

"Please allow me to finish. A few days ago, our aunt wrote to me from London. She is staying at her Grosvenor Street residence for the season for the first time since Cousin Anne's passing."

Sweet Cousin Anne. She had died of consumption not long after my brother's wedding to Elizabeth. Her health had been waning for many years, but my aunt made it no secret that she held my brother somehow responsible for bringing about her untimely death by loving another. Poor Anne, so quiet and unremarkable. Compared to Elizabeth's wit and beauty, she never had a chance to shine, not unlike myself when the Bennet sisters were around.

I banished my feelings of inadequacy and focused again on what my cousin was saying.

"Lady Catherine requested me to extend you her invitation to stay with her in London for the remainder of the season. She believes that your company would be of the utmost comfort and that procuring pleasures for your enjoyment would improve her spirits."

I was certain that Lady Catherine hadn't expressed herself in precisely those words, but I supposed there was ample truth in them. She was indeed going through a difficult time. Re-entering society after two years locked up at Rosings Park couldn't be easy, even for someone as formidable as her. Still, the prospect of spending a few months with my aunt was slightly terrifying.

"I mentioned Lady Catherine's invitation to your brother, but at the time he appeared certain that you would not be willing to leave Mrs Darcy's side so close to her confinement, and therefore he decided it was best not to notify you," continued the Colonel. "However, if Mrs Darcy's health is taking a turn for the worse, it is reasonable to anticipate that her close family members will wish to be by her side."

The Colonel's implication that I was not one of them was distressing, but he did not seem to notice.

"Georgiana, you know as well as I do that Lady Catherine's

relationship with your brother has been somewhat frazzled of late, but she has always esteemed you. Her letter showed her generous and amiable disposition towards you, and an eagerness to provide you with the wider society you require. In my opinion, Lady Catherine's invitation is perfectly timed, and it would be very thoughtful of you to accept her offer and spend time with her in London."

London. I had been at school over there for a short while, but my memories were few and far between. A window overseeing the Thames, a room with high ceilings and little light, a flock of indistinguishable mistresses with very stern faces, all dressed in black.

A red trinket box where I had kept his letters.

I had stayed at the school until Mrs Younge had taken me to Ramsgate. To him. I forcefully pushed Wickham out of my thoughts.

Colonel Fitzwilliam now spoke with the eagerness of those who make plans to improve the life of others.

"Lady Catherine is very well connected, and I have no doubt that she will introduce you to the most elegant and exclusive society. She is also very keen to present you at court, now that she is no longer in deep mourning and it is proper for her to do so."

A court presentation! The elaborate costumes, the nobility, the curtseying to the Queen. My insides shook at the prospect. I found it difficult enough to speak at a dinner party with neighbours in Pemberley. How would I manage to go through the whole ceremony in front of hundreds of people? Of course, I had always known it would happen one day, and in the family it was tacitly understood that, given the tragic death of my mother, my aunt would do the honours. After all, as the daughter of an earl, she had been presented herself, and even spent time at court in her youth. However, since my brother's wedding and Cousin Anne's death, no more had been said on the matter, and I'd harboured the secret fantasy that my dreaded presentation would never actually take place.

"Your brother, always so considerate, feared that the event might bring painful memories of Cousin Anne's coming out to our aunt. Because of this, he insisted on postponing your presentation, and even discussed with me the possibility of looking for a different sponsor."

The Colonel's apologetic tone didn't fool me. I was well aware that Fitzwilliam was anxious about letting me out of his sight. At the same time, I did not mind his watchfulness. I rather enjoyed being cocooned in the safety of Pemberley, and its limited social obligations suited my timid nature.

"However, Lady Catherine is adamant that she will do it herself. She wants your first season to be splendid," continued the Colonel.

I shuddered. There was only one way to determine the social success of a young woman of good breeding in her first full season in town, and that was an engagement to a man with a title or a vast fortune, and preferably both. Cousin Anne was a sad reminder that some ladies, in spite of their wealth, did not attract a husband, presentation at court or not. What if I shared more than Anne's unremarkable looks? What if I, too, was destined never to be loved again and die a spinster, a string of fruitless seasons behind me?

"I think you may find that you enjoy the process more than you think," the Colonel added with a smile. "I am told that the shopping excursions to procure all necessary *accoutrements* for the court ceremony are very pleasurable for the ladies involved. And Lady Catherine has you in very high regard. She often says that you are so similar to Cousin Anne you might have been sisters, certainly the highest of compliments I ever heard her bestow. I have no doubt that our aunt will ensure you have as much amusement and gayness from your stay in town as possible."

Which wasn't much, I thought glumly. Lady Catherine's idea of diversion was to play cards whilst criticising everyone's dress, countenance, habits, skills, house, pets, servants, carriage and general outlook on life.

"Cousin, please tell me. Does my brother not wish me to go to London?" I managed to ask with some effort on my part.

"Not at all, dear Georgiana. Darcy has always known this day would arrive. I keep reminding him that you are no longer a child, but you know what he is like. He does not want any harm to come to you."

Once more, the words were unsaid, but they hurt just the same. I wanted to scream. Instead, I silently dug my nails into the palms of my hands.

"I believe your brother has also had other preoccupations of late. He has been very busy with some matters regarding the estate boundaries. Some neighbouring owner is contesting his right to a particular piece of land or other, but there is no need for you to worry about such matters."

The Colonel took my gloved hand and pressed it.

"Darcy loves you very much, Georgiana, and so do I. We want your happiness. Your brother would like to keep you as a beautiful vase, on a shelf up high, to be seen and never touched, but it is time you went out to see the world. I intend to recommend to him that you accept Lady Catherine's invitation; however, I will not do so without your consent."

His gaze was confident, and it was clear that he did not doubt that I would comply. In truth, I had very little choice. All I could do is nod as he held my arm to help me up the stairs.

Chapter 3

Just as Colonel Fitzwilliam had predicted, Elizabeth's family was quick to announce a visit upon hearing of her malady, and we were readily informed that we were to expect Mr and Mrs Bennet, Mrs Bingley and Mrs Wickham, who was staying with her eldest sister. Fitzwilliam's eyebrows arched upon hearing Lydia's name, but he did not comment on the matter, and neither did I. We both knew how happy Elizabeth would be to see her parents and sisters and, at all events, I was to leave for London shortly. My brother had given his consent to my trip after verifying that I was satisfied with Lady Catherine's designs, and the Pemberley wheels started to turn to make the necessary arrangements for my departure.

The next few days were a blur. Jones, my maidservant, rejoiced at the thought of spending the remainder of the season in town, and took to the task of packing my belongings with earnestness, enthusiastically stressing the virtues of one gown over the other when consulting me as to what needed to be stored into my trunks, between folds of the finest silk paper. She seemed to be particularly worried about my assortment of slippers and made it very clear though frowns and much pointing that I would have to get at least three or four new pairs when I arrived in London as a matter of urgency. I kept nodding and waving vaguely whenever she tried to involve me in any choices. What did I care if she packed the green silk gown or the white muslin one with the blue ribbons if that was all I could decide for myself? I figured that she was able to decide what was required for my trip much better than I did, and let her get on with it.

Whenever I could, I escaped to the garden. I found myself walking more and more these days, as if some of Elizabeth's energy had transferred to my body and I had to exert myself on her behalf. I was finding the late winter air surprisingly uplifting and energising. It was a beautiful time of year to be out. The weather was improving, and the grounds appeared different in each of my walks. More and more leaves and flowers, like nosy little creatures, were beginning emerging from their buds, slowly coming out of their wintry shells. Some of the birds that had left in the autumn were back already, their song joining that of the robin and the sparrow. I was deeply sorry to be departing just as the spring delights were beginning at Pemberley, and regardless of how hard I tried to convince myself that the joys of city life would make me soon forget about the country, the sadness remained.

The guests arrived right before luncheon on the first Tuesday in March. I saw the Bingley's carriage approach in the distance, its large size announcing the comfortable lifestyle of its owners. I was sitting on the bench by the pond, resting after a bracing walk in the garden, and upon the sight I felt every muscle in my body tense, as if I were a hound getting ready for the hunt. The only time I had met Mrs Wickham I had made a fool of myself, but this time I was ready.

I stood up, grabbed my parasol and headed towards the house, my head held high. Upon entering, I checked my image in the large looking-glass in the hallway to ensure I looked my best. The light breeze had undone the tightest pins in my hair, and fragile wisps had come loose, but there was no time to get them fixed. I tamed the curls around my face as best I could with my fingers. Then, with hands clasped, I went out into the glaring midday sun to welcome the visitors. My brother was standing by the front entrance, his back perfectly straight, his brow creased. When he saw me, he gave me a faint smile.

As we were waiting for the carriage to approach, I thought about Mrs Wickham. Elizabeth may or may not have sensed my dislike of her youngest sister, but I had the feeling that the lady herself was perfectly aware of it. Lydia Wickham was pretty and full of grace, but the spell was broken the moment she opened her mouth: her conversation was stupid and self-centered, just like her mother's, but where Mrs Bennet was foolish, her youngest daughter was becoming an artful and a malicious gossip, no doubt encouraged by some of the dubious company the Wickhams enjoyed. Nevertheless, what irked me was that Lydia, like all naturally lucky people, took her good fortune for granted. She had beauty, the affection of her parents and sisters and the hand of the only man I had ever loved. I, on the contrary, was doubly an orphan, and a plain-looking one at that, who had loved and lost for want of courage, and may never love again.

How can life be so unfair? Why should all fortune be hers?

The carriage approached the main building and finally came to a stop. A footman in the Bingley livery jumped to open the glossy door, and a delicate, gloved hand came out, expecting assistance to be dispensed. My brother's impeccable manners took over his natural reserve, and he promptly offered his services to the lady. It was Mrs Wickham.

Lydia seemed to be getting more alluring with age, as she approached the peak of natural bloom in young women. Her eyes were dark, very much Elizabeth's, but without her sister's spark and kindness. In Mrs Wickham's features, so familiar yet so strange at the same time, they appeared injudicious and derisive. Her demeanour was different, too, more polished than I remembered.

My brother gave Mrs Wickham a short welcome, and her reply quickly turned into a long monologue about the unpleasantness of late winter weather. She then proceeded to order her parents and eldest sister to come out of the coach with a loud cry and an imperious gesture. Lydia had clearly decided to take the role of expedition leader. I saw my brother's neck redden, a rare and ominous sign.

Mr Bennet had his usual distracted air. He greeted Fitzwilliam warmly but his mind was somewhere else, and I had no doubt that he would rush to hide in the library at the first occasion, as was his habit whenever he visited Pemberley. His wife, better known for her ability to speak without a pause on the most uninteresting matters, was quieter than usual, perhaps due to the natural worries of a mother faced with the indisposition of one of her offspring. Mrs Bingley, the Bennet sister I had become most acquainted to and loved best, was her usual gentle self, but I noticed she looked overburdened. I wondered if Wickham had joined his wife at Mr and Mrs Bingley's home, and considered it likely. I knew through the sources that managed to avoid my brother's scrutiny that he often stayed with the Bingleys when his wife was visiting her eldest sister. Mr and Mrs Bingley were too kind-hearted to refuse an appeal to their generosity.

After giving the guests some time to refresh themselves, we met them again in the front drawing room. The nursemaid brought down her young charge, and my nephew Will quickly became the centre of attention, delighting his grandparents and aunts with his affectionate embraces and his adorable demeanour. He was not yet a toddler of two, but he was already quite a personality. My brother made the most of the situation to excuse himself, alluding to some estate business that he had to attend to and giving his assurances that he would be back in time to join the family for dinner. With my brother gone, Mrs Bennet became visibly more relaxed and so did Mrs Wickham, if such a thing was possible. We briefly conversed about their journey and the state of the local roads. Mrs Wickham was very vocal.

"That coach of yours may be new and shiny and covered in the softest velvet, Jane, but the road feels so much bumpier than in Colonel Slater's carriage. His is much more utilitarian, of course, it being just leather mounted on horse's hair, but Mrs Slater and I agree that it is possibly the most agreeable means to be taken from place to place. Don't you think, Mama?"

Before Mrs Bennet could reply Mrs Bingley, who had young Will on her lap, intervened.

"Now tell us, Miss Darcy, how is Mrs Darcy and when can we see her?" she asked with an anguished look on his face.

I swallowed.

"She is still rather unwell, I'm afraid. Dr Robertson has instructed that Elizabeth may only see a visitor or two a day at the most, as it is essential not to excite her."

Mrs Bingley put her hand on my arm.

"Miss Darcy, we are all very keen to speak to her, as you would expect, but we understand the physician's orders," she said softly. "Mama, shall you and I go into Elizabeth's sick room today, and Papa and Lydia can see her tomorrow?"

"And why should *I* have to wait until tomorrow?" Mrs Wickham intervened, with the tone of a four-year-old fighting over a toy. "I'm her sister as well, you know, and I have been married far longer than you, so if anything I am entitled to go in *before* you."

Mrs Bingley stared at her youngest sister in shock but quickly recovered her composure.

"Miss Darcy, have you had the chance to see Mrs Darcy in the last couple of days?" she asked, handing Will to his grandmother.

"Unfortunately not. She has been very feeble and in need of rest, and I did not wish to disturb her."

"And I understand that you are departing for London soon, are you not? Mr Darcy mentioned it in his most recent letter."

"Indeed, I am, Mrs Bingley. I am leaving tomorrow."

"Let Mama visit Elizabeth today with Miss Darcy, and Lydia and I can both go tomorrow," ruled Mrs Bingley. "I am sure Papa will not mind."

Mrs Wickham turned to look at me from the first time since her arrival. She had studiously ignored me until then, and her behaviour had suited me fine, but now I was the object of her most unrepressed interest. She observed my curled hair, my face, my nose, my jaw. Her gaze descended to my neck, where it lingered on the diamond cross that sat between my collar bones. She took in my bust, my pale blue muslin dress, my hands, gently folded on my lap as Mrs Annesley always insisted. She continued down the outline of my legs, sketched by the soft fabric, to finish with my brocaded satin slippers. Then she gave me a strange smile, a disconcerting mix of annoyance, indifference and envy.

"Certainly."

Mrs Bingley coloured deeply but, the matter settled, she didn't say anything.

The conversation moved on to Miss Bennet and Miss Catherine Bennet, who were staying with Mr and Mrs Gardiner in Cheapside. They had been there for a couple of weeks, and they would probably remain in London for the rest of the season. Mrs Bennet, who had been bouncing Will on her knee, immediately intervened.

"I do hope you will see Mary and Kitty in London, Miss Darcy," she said eagerly. "You know that my brother keeps a *very* elegant house in town, don't you? It's on Gracechurch street, a *most* respectable address."

I was aware of that. In fact, I knew the Gardiners rather well, on account of their having visited Pemberley on several occasions. They were a charming couple and had always been agreeable to me. I would be delighted to visit them in town, even if I didn't find the Misses Bennet particularly interesting. Mary was an educated fool, the worst kind, and had very few charms to recommend her. Kitty was dangerously similar to Lydia, although she'd been reigned in before becoming too wild. Such was the general understanding, anyway.

"I would be delighted, Mrs Bennet, provided that Lady Catherine de Bourgh approves. I will be staying with her."

Silence ensued. Mrs Bingley's countenance remained calm, but Mrs Bennet was visibly affected by my words and even Mrs

Wickham's pretty face lost some of its colour. Only Mr Bennet remained oblivious to my remark. If I had ever doubted that my formidable aunt was capable of striking fear in others' hearts, their reactions settled it. I felt a tingle of pleasure before excusing myself to go and find the nurse with Mrs Bennet.

* * *

The visit to the sickroom was as awkward as such occasions tend to be. Elizabeth was under the bedcover in the big bed she shared with my brother, a silver tray with some soup at her feet. Even in the darkness of the room, with the velvet curtains half drawn, she looked very drained. When we went in, she smiled in our direction, and if she was disappointed to see it was me accompanying her mother instead of her sister Jane, she didn't show it.

Mrs Bennet was all teary eyes and grasping hands, her concern rather overwhelming to all who witnessed it, starting with the patient. Although she was clearly weak, Elizabeth had to do most of the comforting, rather than the other way around. After assuring her mother that she wasn't about to die, my sister-in-law turned towards me.

"Dear Georgiana, it's so lovely that you came to visit. Have you been outside? It's a beautiful day, from what I've been allowed to glimpse."

Elizabeth waved at the curtains with a resigned, graceful

gesture. She was a naturally vivacious person, but very little of her usual sparkle seemed left in her, and her words, spoken at a much slower pace than usual, caused me some alarm. I answered with a brief account of my morning walk, but my expression must have betrayed my concern, because she gave me a tired smile.

"You must not worry about me when you're in London, Georgiana. Dr Robertson was here yesterday, and he seemed satisfied, or as satisfied as he can ever be, with my evolution. Mama, Miss Darcy will have told you that the physician has given the sternest instructions as to what I am to do and not do until the baby is born. I do not agree with some of his advice, but he seems to have Mr Darcy's full confidence and support, and I just don't have the spirit to contradict them."

Another arm wave. This time I saw the marks of the bloodletting sessions on her wrists and shuddered.

I stayed for a while longer. Mrs Bennet didn't give me much of a chance to intervene in the ensuing conversation, but it comforted me to see that my sister-in-law's sense of humour was intact in spite of her ill health. When I noticed that the patient was getting fatigued, and announced my intention to leave, Elizabeth took my hand in hers with an eagerness that surprised me. I realised that, in spite of her composure, she was afraid of the possible outcomes for her and the baby. I pressed her hand, trying to convey in gestures, more than words, my confidence in her strength to overcome the evils of illness and the dangers of childbirth. Her mother, of course, didn't pay any attention to what was right in front of her eyes.

"Lizzy, you really are *so* brave. Anyone in your condition would be worried sick of what might occur, but look at *you*, feeble but in good spirits! You remember what happened to Maria, the youngest Lucas girl, don't you? That's Mrs Collins' sister for you, Miss Darcy, in case you know her. Oh, it was a tragedy, indeed! Such a nice young woman. Not a beauty like mine, of course – Lord knows that the Lucas girls are all rather plain– but she made a good match, married a very respectable gentleman and settled not far from Longbourn, just a short ride from her parents, as it ought to be. She had every reason for happiness, really. Then she started having troubles–"

Elizabeth must have given her a severe look, because Mrs Bennet suddenly twisted her mouth and went quiet for once.

Before leaving the sick chamber, Elizabeth made me promise I would see her younger sisters in London. This time I really could not refuse. Lady Catherine or not, I would have to find a way to visit the Misses Bennet. I quietly closed the door behind me and went downstairs, where Elizabeth's sisters were awaiting my news, Jane with genuine concern and Lydia with a great deal of unnecessary drama. I was updating them on the health of the patient when Mrs Bennet stormed into the drawing room.

"That horrible woman! Would you believe she had the nerve to tell *me* that Elizabeth needed some rest? As if I didn't know my own daughter! Miss Darcy, I do hope you will have a word with her. Her behaviour was quite inexcusable."

"Is that so, Mama? I cannot believe it! And working for such wealthy people, too! How impertinent!" echoed Lydia, if anything even more incensed than her mother.

"Mrs Bennet, Mrs Wickham, I'm afraid the nurse is simply following Dr Robertson's instructions, and you can rest assured that Mrs Darcy's wellbeing is his only concern. But you shall be able to speak to him shortly; he usually visits her at about this time."

As if on cue, the doorbell rang and Dr Robertson made an appearance in the drawing room shortly afterwards. After the briefest of introductions, and as if anticipating Mrs Bennet's objections, Dr Robertson started off on a soliloquy about the dangers of overexertion in mothers-to-be that was peppered with medical terms. His knowledge must have impressed Mrs Bennet, for she quickly adopted a meek attitude in contrast to Lydia's still belligerent mood. Making the most of the confusion, I excused myself and escaped to my bedchamber. Dinner was only a couple of hours away and I was determined to show my brother how capable I was of playing the perfect hostess.

Chapter 4

That night, Pemberley was to welcome a party of twelve. On the guest list were Elizabeth's relatives, Colonel Fitzwilliam and Dr Robertson and his wife, a nervous woman who didn't say much and seemed startled by anything. We were also joined by our neighbours, Reverend Walker, Mrs Walker and their only son, Mr Donald Walker. The reverend was gaunt and very tall, with a squint and prematurely grey hair. His wife, matronly and opinionated, had a high-pitched voice that could be heard from across the room and which she enjoyed exercising. I didn't much care for Mrs Walker, who was a ruthless gossip, but I quite liked the reverend. He tended to be quiet when his wife was around but he was widely read and eager to share his knowledge with the right listener. I was mildly intrigued by Mr Walker. I had never met him before, but I knew through his parents that he had completed his studies of law and his prospects were excellent. Perhaps I would gain an admirer that night.

In Elizabeth's absence, my place would be beside my brother for most of the evening. I had prepared with great care and was wearing an *eau-de-nil* gown with yellow ribbons that Jones had assured me was very becoming. She had curled my hair in a different way, perhaps inspired by Lydia's coiffure. It was vexing that it had taken the visit of my least favourite woman bar Mrs Younge to nudge her into trying a new hairstyle, but I was too pleased with the results to say anything. The curls framed my face and softened my features most pleasingly. The gown was my idea; I had it made for Elizabeth and Fitzwilliam's wedding celebrations but hadn't worn it much since. It was too pale for winter, but now that the weather was becoming warmer it was the perfect outfit.

I looked out of the window, which framed a delightful sky. The vivid sun was low on the horizon, colouring the clouds a beautiful shade of pink. I drew a deep breath and headed downstairs. Mrs Wickham and Mrs Bennet were already waiting in the drawing room, standing by the roaring fire. Mrs Bennet was wearing a green gown and embroidered shawl that Elizabeth had gifted her for Christmas, and her youngest daughter was clad in a scarlet dress that suited her slender figure. Mother and daughter turned to greet me when they heard my footsteps.

I almost gasped when I saw Mrs Wickham's gown. The cut was very tight, much more so than the fashions I was used to seeing in Pemberley, and featured a very low *décolletage*, barely covered with a hint of dark lace. She noticed my shock with an arch smile. Then the library door opened and Mr Bennet reluctantly joined us. Fitzwilliam and the Colonel followed from the other direction shortly afterwards. They had been in private conversation in the study for an hour and seemed troubled and tense.

At the agreed hour on the dot, the doorbell rang to announce the arrival of the Walkers. To my delight, the young Mr Walker was taller than me, and had an agreeable countenance, even if the skin on his face was ravaged by pimples. He smiled at me when we were introduced and seemed very pleased to make my acquaintance. Then he spotted Lydia, and his scarred skin coloured violently, the fleshy craters practically disappearing in the pinkness of his face. Judging by her flirtatious smile, Mrs Wickham was delighted by the impact she had had on him. Reverend Walker was her next victim. Even before they had spoken she fluttered her eyelashes at the poor man, and his errant eye started to roam widely, like a ship with no compass. Unaware, Mrs Walker was busy regaling everyone about the precise details of her morning trip to Lambton.

"And I said to Dr Robertson, as we'll be at Pemberley later, will you be so kind as to give Mrs Darcy *permission* to dine with us? I said it in jest, Dr Robertson knows how I like to tease, but he was as serious as usual. Then I remarked, 'I don't like the way you're staring at me, Dr Robertson, I hope you haven't made poor Mrs Darcy *that* unwell'."

"I assure you that's not the case, Mrs Walker," my brother interjected, his voice laced with irritation. "My wife just needs some rest. You will remember Mr and Mrs Bennet, of course. I believe you have also met Mrs Bingley. And this is Mrs–"

Fitzwilliam looked at Lydia, then winced. His neck started to turn a distinct shade of crimson. I held my breath.

"–Wickham! You must be the youngest sister!" exclaimed Mrs Walker, unable to contain herself. "Where is your charming husband, pray tell me? I haven't seen him in a long time!"

All the other small talk in the room abruptly stopped at the mention of Wickham. Mrs Bennet seemed to perk up at the glowing mention of her son-in-law. My brother was livid. Colonel Fitzwilliam, ever the expert at defusing sensitive situations, stepped in.

"Mrs Bennet, Mrs Walker, I must take advantage of having such experienced ladies in my presence to ask you for some advice on household management," he said with his usual charm. "As you are well aware, I am a poor bachelor with numerous responsibilities, and it is increasingly taxing for me to find the time and energy to manage my servants. I have a faithful housekeeper who has been with me many years, but I fear some of the duties are proving too much for her. What would you recommend me to do?"

Mrs Walker was quick to bite the bait.

"Oh, but Colonel Fitzwilliam, you *must* marry! A dutiful wife will ensure your household runs like clockwork. I have two pretty nieces, very accomplished and dutiful as well, I must introduce you to. They live in Yorkshire, but I will ask them to visit."

"Kitty is *so* skilled at instructing our Longbourn servants, Colonel. So much so, that I need to do very little by way of supervision. She has grown much since the last time you saw her, and she is turning into a rather beautiful young woman. I have already asked Miss Darcy, but promise me that you will meet her and Mary when you are in town. She will be delighted to see you!"

Colonel Fitzwilliam's intervention gave me the chance to regain my composure. I gave my cousin a silent look of thanks, which he acknowledged with a barely-there nod, and I proceeded to invite our guests to adjourn to the dining room.

It was an uneasy evening. My brother was on edge, a look of preoccupation clouding his noble features. I didn't think it was solely due to Mrs Wickham's coquettishness. He found her irritating, that was sure, but I sensed there was something else. Colonel Fitzwilliam led the conversation and charmed the ladies, seated as he was between Mrs Bennet and Mrs Walker. I believe that night he learnt enough about servant management to write a full volume on the matter.

I was sitting between Mr Bennet and Reverend Walker, who turned out to have a shared love of knowledge and learning. Reflecting their scholarly interests, their conversation, moved from a recent fossil discovery to piston steam engines. They were so enthused in their exchange that most of the time they failed to notice me, only remarking occasionally, 'Isn't it so, Miss Darcy?'

Across from me, Lydia was talking animatedly with Mr Walker, touching his sleeve more than was seemly for any well-bred woman, let alone a married one. As for Mr Walker, he was so in awe of Mrs Wickham in general, and of her bosom in particular, that he barely said anything. My spirits sank. He wasn't exactly a handsome man, his facial scarring was too severe, but it would have been nice to have male attention for a while. And he did have lovely lips, now drawing a hint of a smile. They were shapely and firm, like Wickham's.

The memories came flooding in, unexpectedly. The smell of soap on his cheeks. The way Wickham smiled at me when he said that he loved me. The strength of his arms when he had lifted me up the day before our planned elopement. 'Next time I do this, you shall be my wife', he had said. How could Lydia be here when she had him at home? My heart ached deeply, taking my breath away. I must have gasped because all of a sudden everyone was looking at me.

"Are you well, Miss Darcy?" enquired the reverend, his voice tinged with worry.

"Quite well, I thank you", I mumbled.

From his seat at the top of the table, my brother was observing me with concern. I smiled bravely in his direction, took a deep breath, straightened my back, as Mrs Annesley always said I should do, and invited the ladies to follow me back to the drawing room. As we were walking along the corridor, Mrs Wickham approached me.

"I hope you do not fall ill, Miss Darcy. It won't do your looks any favour, and you will need what little you have if you are to find a husband."

She giggled, covering her mouth with her delicate hand. I turned around. None of the other ladies seemed to have taken notice of her comment. Mrs Bennet and Mrs Walker were engrossed in discussing the difficulty of finding skilled cooks, the viciousness of old servants and the lack of attention to detail of scullery maids. Mrs Bingley appeared distracted, perhaps worried about her sister, and Mrs Robertson was silently walking by her side with her usual vacant look, content with her role of mute guest. With my cheeks burning, I went through to the next room feeling, not for the first time since the arrival of the Bennets, that I was of little or no consequence in Pemberley when my brother and sister-in-law weren't present.

I sat at the pianoforte and began to play. Lydia's malice had thrown me in a state of anger and shame that was swiftly becoming deep sorrow. I was so desolate that the tune of my choice must have sounded too mournful for my audience, for Mrs Bennet shortly after asked me to perform something more lively. I obeyed without saying a word. A while later, the men entered the room, and there was a discreet scramble for places. Mrs Walker insisted that everyone should sit down for a game of loo, and Mrs Bennet took up the suggestion with enthusiasm. Mr Bennet didn't agree, however.

"My dear, I would like Reverend Walker to see a most

extraordinary sixteenth-century copy of a sketch showing the workings of an *architonnerre* that Mr Darcy is lucky enough to have in his excellent library. I'm sure you'll understand that one must bow to the greatness of Leonardo whenever one has the chance. Mr Darcy, I hope you will indulge us and share with us this unique example of engineering ingenuity."

My brother, as a good host and proud owner of some remarkable works, gladly acquiesced. He and the older men, excited like school children and clearly pleased to escape the card table, promptly left the room.

Colonel Fitzwilliam suggested that instead of loo a pool of commerce would be preferable, given the number of players.

"Georgiana will be kind enough to continue to delight us with her playing, I'm sure," he added.

I silently thanked my cousin. He knew how little I cared for cards.

"What a wonderful idea!" exclaimed Mrs Wickham. "Mr Walker, you sit right there. Mama, you sit next to him; Jane, take the seat to Mr Walker's left; and Mrs Walker, you must sit here, by my side. And Colonel Fitzwilliam, I must admit that I am rather inept at cards, so I hope you will take pity on me. Would you be able to fetch the chair over there to sit next to me and show me how to improve my game as we go along?"

Just like that, Lydia managed to secure my cousin's attention through the duration of the card game whilst also keeping that of Mr Walker, who appeared very pleased to be able to take full advantage of the perspective that a seat across from Mrs Wickham afforded him.

The game of commerce soon became quite absorbing, judging by the little conversation that was taking place amongst the players, to the point that Mrs Wickham seemed to forget that she was supposed to ask Colonel Fitzwilliam for his advice. Not that I cared. Instead, I focused on the joy of feeling the keys under my fingers. I had learnt to play at a young age, and through the years the pianoforte had become a fixed constant in my life. The instrument was a source of great comfort in times of distress, such as the wake of Wickham's departure.

Wickham.

The pang in my heart was a faint echo of what it had been. I had loved him deeply and believed him when he said that he loved me in return. I considered him to be a dependable and trustworthy companion, a deserving recipient of my affections. Only he wasn't. And he was now married to a stupid and impudent woman who was more interested in displaying her charms to other men than in living with him in marital bliss.

Why is she blessed with good fortune? Why not me?

I felt the familiar tingling behind my eyes.

Not now.

Nobody seemed to notice my distress. The card players were immersed in their game. My cousin I couldn't see, but I suspected he must have excused himself to join the rest of the men in the library. I took a deep breath and focused on my fingertips, feeling the ivory yield graciously under my touch. Little by little, I lost myself in the music. I don't consider myself to be a particularly gifted player, and I am aware that my skill is more due to the regular practice instigated by Mrs Annesley than to natural talent, but I bow to the power of a musical instrument to soothe the spirit and erase everything else in the world.

I heard the door open. The men must be back in the room.

The piece was ending, flowing through my fingers like water. From the corner of my eye, I could see a male figure standing behind me, waiting for me to finish. My brother, probably. I played the final key. The gentleman clapped gently, and I turned around. It was cousin Fitzwilliam.

"That was a beautiful performance, Georgiana. Your skills are much improved since my last visit. Do you practise more often these days? Perhaps you have a new music tutor."

Mrs Wickham's scream stilled my answer on my lips.

"Colonel, where are you? Did you see? I've won!"

Lydia came towards us. Her eyes were shining and in her palm was a bunch of coins. She grabbed my cousin's arm with her free hand and shook it.

"Can you believe my good fortune? I needed it to make up for your lack of assistance, Colonel. I did not notice you leave my side until the end of the game. Fancy hovering over the pianoforte instead of helping *me*!"

The claws of envy mauled my insides but I tried to remain composed.

The evening slowly came to a close. The Walkers and the Robertsons departed an hour later, and Elizabeth's relatives retired to their rooms shortly afterwards. My brother, who was in the library with Colonel Fitzwilliam, called for me as I was going up the stairs to my room. He was standing by the fireplace, lost in the dancing of the flames. The Colonel was sitting down on one of the armchairs, a glass of whisky in his hand. When my cousin saw me, he smiled and coughed to draw my brother's attention. Fitzwilliam looked at me with tired but kind eyes.

"My dear Georgiana, I must apologise for keeping you from your bed. You must be fatigued; it has been a long day, and you have an early start tomorrow, so I will be brief. I am deeply sorry, but I will not be able to join you in London as initially planned. The issue concerning the estate boundaries requires my presence."

Here he stopped, and hesitated, then went on.

"Moreover, I have grown increasingly concerned about Mrs Darcy. After much consideration, I have come to the conclusion that my duty at the moment is to stay in Pemberley."

His eyes were glazed, as if a fine layer of ice had set over them since dinner. I wondered whether it was the whisky. He quickly regained his composure and extended his arm towards the Colonel.

"However, Colonel Fitzwilliam, in his usual attentive fashion, has kindly offered to escort you to Grosvenor Square and ensure that you are comfortably settled with Lady Catherine before taking leave."

The Colonel lifted his glass in my direction.

"Georgiana, you know how important your happiness and wellbeing are to me, and my affection is what drives me to tell you what I'm about to say," continued my brother with some embarrassment. "I am sure you realise that you are a remarkably attractive prospect to men of all sorts for a variety of reasons, and I entreat you to be careful in the extreme."

A reminder of my past behaviour. I blushed. It had been five long years, but I still caught the odd glance between my brother and my cousin. It pained me to see that the self-command and poise that I had worked hard to cultivate weren't enough to make up for the much-regretted lapse in judgement of my early youth.

Noticing my downcast gaze, my brother put a hand on my arm and squeezed it softly. He had started doing it on occasion when Elizabeth had become Mrs Darcy, and I suspected the events were connected; quite simply, she softened him. As a result of his wife's influence, he had begun
to demonstrate his affection more outwardly since his wife came into our lives, and I was not one to complain about it.

My cousin stood up and came towards us.

"I will be ready before dawn, Georgiana. London awaits us."

Chapter 5

The days were still short, and I was not used to travelling, so the Colonel decided that it was best to split the journey into three days. It would be much less fatiguing for me, he insisted, and he would not hear otherwise, although I would have much preferred to risk some discomfort and get to London a day earlier. We were due to depart at the crack of dawn. The drumming of the rain and the excitement about the impending journey had arisen me in the early hours, well before Jones was due to awaken me, and I had been unable to go back to sleep. My temples pounded with the fear of leaving Pemberley after all these years, mixed with the dizzying prospect of adventure that may await me in London. Marriage could well be on the cards, perhaps romance as well, and the notion was intoxicating.

When Jones finally entered my room with a candle in her

hands, she found me ready to leave. Shortly afterwards I was being rattled about inside the cushioned and velvety walls of the carriage, drops of water relentlessly hitting its roof. We drove past countryside that was barely visible, so faint was the first light of the morning. Even when daylight came, the rain was so thick and the drops covering the carriage windows so big that it was difficult to see what was outside. From my seat, all I could discern were naked branches, big puddles and grey mist beyond the side of the road. It was icy cold, and I was grateful to Elizabeth for insisting I took the grey fur blanket that usually sat at the foot of her bed.

Perhaps the change in the weather brought about a melancholy feeling, but Colonel Fitzwilliam was unusually silent. I had always regarded him as the charming and gay counterpoint to my brother's natural reserve and propriety, but for once his company was predictable and rather dull. I noticed grey hairs were outnumbering his natural shade. He was a few years older than Fitzwilliam, but he had not yet married. Until the end of the war, military life had shielded him from the usual troubles of the second son, but now the conflict was over, there was no escaping the fact that he had no fortune to offer to his future bride. I wondered if this was what was troubling him.

The only event to break up the long journey south were the stops. Roadside inns proved to be as entertaining as I remembered all those years ago, and they never failed to provide a wide range of fascinating characters. There were tradespeople, travelling up and down the country to offer their wares; lawyers, civil servants and other men in similar professions, distinguishable by their sober yet expensive clothing, and unusually discreet in their manners. There were ladies and gentlemen on similar journeys to ours, heading to London for the season and enduring the discomfort of the experience, all wrapped up in fine furs and woollen blankets. There were also groups of working men of all ages and families travelling in large groups, loud and unbridled, merry and shouty, jealous and generous. At the first roadside inn, it was impossible to obtain a private room for our meals, so I had a few opportunities to get quite close to some of these characters and even discreetly eavesdrop on their conversations. Their stories, delivered in accents that bewildered me, were always intriguing, and their coarse voices broke the dullness of the trip and the lacklustre conversation of my companion.

At an inn, one day from our destination, I had an even more intimate encounter with a member of the lower classes. We arrived just before dark, under a slate grey sky. It had been raining since we set off in the morning, and the whole inn courtyard was one immense puddle with inches deep of mud. The driver opened the door, and the Colonel got out. He groaned, and I looked out of the window, through the thick rain. My cousin was standing precariously on a broken wooden plank smeared in mud that someone had left on the filthy courtyard, presumably to help travellers reach the safety of the inn door.

"Georgiana, it would be best if you stayed inside the carriage for the moment. I will go inside and find some help."

And with those words, he left.

The pitter-patter of the rain wasn't easing off. If anything, it was drumming the roof of the carriage with more insistence than ever. I was eager to stretch my legs, but my cousin had been clear: I was to wait for him. Outside, I could only see darkness beyond the smeared glass.

All of a sudden, something hit the carriage at a great speed, and I was thrown onto the floor like a rag doll. The cab tilted, and for a split second I thought it would overturn. In the confusion, something hit my head hard, right on the hairline. I instinctively covered it my hand, too late to avoid the blow.

The footman! Where is the footman?

And where is the Colonel?

A feeling of dizziness invaded my whole being, and I realised that the fingers I had wrapped around the edge of my forehead were wet.

Blood.

Far away, as in a dream, I heard screams and a man shouting, asking if anybody was in the carriage. I wanted to answer, but my voice was gone. Then, there was a loud bang on the door of the carriage.

Here comes another one.

I braced myself for a second blow.

After a struggle, someone opened the door of the vehicle.

"Are you hurt, madam?"

I tried to respond, but I could only manage a whimper.

The stranger climbed onto the carriage. I slowly opened my eyes, but all I could see in the darkness was a large shadow approaching me. As my sight got used to the little light that poured through from the windows, I beheld a tall man with a straight nose and a strong jaw. He was standing still, appraising the graveness of the situation. When he saw that my eyes were open, he seemed to shudder, and promptly took my wrist. His hand was solid and warm. I didn't realise until later, when I had run the events several times in my head, that he was checking my pulse. When he seemed satisfied, he touched my forehead, and immediately noticed the blood. Then, with a kind voice, he started to whisper soothing words, as you would to an injured animal or lost child. I closed my eyes again, allowing the sounds to calm me.

With a deft movement, he lifted me up, resting my head against his chest. His coat smelled of horse, wet wool and tobacco. His grip was gentle, but his strength surprised me; in his arms, I felt weightless, a mere feather of a woman. In my shocked state, I remember thinking that he must be some kind of strongman, someone who earned a living lifting cattle in rickety roadside shows and country fairs. I had never been to one myself, but I had overheard many excited conversations from the lowlier servants and village residents about the wonders one could observe at such events in exchange for a few coins.

Outside, the rain drops were falling with such force that the noise they made muffled the commotion in the courtyard. Two men were shouting at each other; a third one was trying to pacify them. In the background, a horse was groaning.

The stranger was humming now, his chin very close to my forehead. I felt the rain relentlessly pour down from the skies on my face and body. Then, my feet gently touched the flagstones of the inn.

I was safe.

I looked up. My saviour was younger than I expected, just a few years my senior, and was wearing a long overcoat and hat which had seen better days. He was as tall as Fitzwilliam, but where my brother had the grace and elegance conferred by gentlemanly pursuits, the stranger exuded a raw strength that spoke of vigorous physical activity. He also had piercing blue eyes.

My head was spinning, and I was breathless, but it wasn't an unpleasant feeling. Quite the opposite.

I allowed the man to guide me towards the hearth and seat me by the fire. Then, he handed me a hip flask.

"Drink some; it will do you good. You are in shock."

I took a sip. The liquid burnt my insides, but it also jolted me back to reality. The stranger had a worried look on his face.

"I beg you to allow me to have a look at your forehead, madam."

I touched the cut with my fingers.

"It's nothing," I muttered.

"I must insist. I have some medical training."

He gently pulled my curls back with the palm of his hand, so that he could have an interrupted view of my temple.

"There is a lot of blood, madam, but it's nothing serious," he said after a few moments. "The wound does not require any stitches, and it will heal of its own accord if you keep it clean and aired. You should also apply some strong wine the first few times to close it, although I wouldn't trust what you will be served in this place."

He frowned, then smiled.

"Here, keep this," he said, placing his hip flask in my hands. "Use the liquid on the wound. It will sting to begin with, but it will help it heal better."

I objected, but he wouldn't hear of it. Then, I noticed some hesitation on his behalf. The drink had given me confidence, and I boldly asked him whether there was something else he wanted to add.

"It's just that the injury may leave a scar, madam. One so small you will be hardly able to see it, I assure you, but a scar nevertheless."

"It will be a small price to pay to come out of such a frightening incident unharmed. I thought that my time had arrived. Please, sir, can you tell me what happened?"

My saviour seemed surprised with my lack of concern about the markings the injury may leave on my skin. He gave me a half-smile and then his countenance became serious.

"An old horse slipped in the mud and the landau the poor beast was dragging banged against your carriage. You are lucky it didn't turn, or your cut could have been a much more severe concussion."

I savoured the word.

Lucky.

For once, that had been me.

"I thank you, sir, for your assistance. It was–"

A voice interrupted me.

"Georgiana, dearest, here you are at last! Are you well?"

Colonel Fitzwilliam had appeared out of nowhere, a preoccupied look on his face. He firmly caught my hands between his.

"I bet she is better now than she would have been otherwise," said the stranger, visibly more relaxed than he had been just a few minutes earlier.

Cousin Fitzwilliam stared at him with steely eyes.

"I thank you, but that is for us to decide."

He fumbled in his pocket and extended a hand towards the stranger. The young man did the same, and I thought they would shake hands, but instead, the Colonel put something in my saviour's palm. The stranger stared at it and shook his head in disbelief, his eyes wide. Then I realised. My cousin had dropped two half-sovereigns in his palm. A tight smile appeared on my saviour's lips. He looked at the coins once more, hesitated, then closed his fist around them.

"It has been too much of a pleasure to assist this lady to take offence at your words," he said with great dignity. "Good night, sir. Madam –"

With a bow, the stranger disappeared inside the darkness of the inn, leaving my cousin speechless. Perhaps it was an effect of the flickering light, but I could have sworn the man winked at me before he took his leave.

That night we had a private dining room with a roaring fire. As soon as it was possible, Jones cleaned my wound with the spirit in the hip flask the stranger had given me. With every drop of liquid, a thousand needles pierced my skin, but, once clean, the laceration turned out to be much smaller than anticipated. It was barely the size of my smallest fingernail. I smiled. Everything would be fine, just as the stranger had promised.

I sensed the attraction building inside of me. What lady could prevent admiring her saviour in circumstances such as the ones I had experienced, if only out of gratitude? However, I willed myself to forget the man's kind face. It was foolish to entertain any fantasies about my rescuer. Judging by his attire, he was my social inferior by many rungs. And yet, his manners, his gentleness, his behaviour, were those of a gentleman. Had he not said he had medical training of some kind? Perhaps he was a dresser, or a medical student, although this didn't quite explain the rusticity of his dress.

During the meal, I was in a haze of horse and wool and tobacco, and couldn't bring myself to say much. My cousin attributed my silence to the shock of the incident in the courtyard and proceeded to give me the particulars of what had happened, as explained to him by the inn owner. Apparently, it wasn't the first time that this kind of occurrence had taken place. It was always the same coachman, a local driver who occasionally took too much to drink and whose horse was getting too old for a reckless master, especially in treacherous weather.

The Colonel didn't mention the stranger, and neither did I, but as we were eating, and the muffled sounds of the main dining rooms reached us through the gaps in the floorboards that weren't covered by the tattered carpet, I wondered where exactly in the bowels of the inn the stranger would be at that precise moment.

Chapter 6

We arrived in London the following afternoon. It had stopped raining, and the roads in the south were substantially better than they had been further north, so we found ourselves outside the grand entrance of my aunt's Grosvenor Square residence well before twilight. Two men in livery immediately stepped out through the shiny black front door, and we were ushered inside. We were informed that Lady Catherine was out but should be back soon. It was a relief to have some time to myself. I changed into fresh clothes and sat on the bed in the room my aunt had chosen for me. It was almost as large as my bedchamber in Pemberley but so full of carved furniture, ornaments, tapestries and curtains that it appeared considerably smaller.

I opened one of my trunks and drew the hip flask out. In the poor light of the inn I had taken it to be made out of pewter, but now I wasn't so sure. I rubbed it with my petticoat and the dull surface gave way to shiny metal. Silver, then. I took the object closer to the large window to have a better look. It was well used, and had clearly seen a lot of action, with plenty of bumps and scratches as testament of an adventurous life. Certainly, its owner was not idle. The mystery surrounding the identity of my saviour appeared unsolvable. If only I had a name...

Something on the surface of the flask grabbed my attention. I looked closely. There was an inscription of some kind. I rubbed some more with my petticoat. It was small, but legible: *W.P.* Right below the initial there was a date, etched in the same plain script: *10/04/1810.*

There was a knock on the door; with a quick movement I hid the hip flask in my pocket. It was a maid informing me that Lady Catherine was back and was waiting for me downstairs. I nodded, expecting to have some time to myself so as to put the object back into the trunk, but the servant stood there, clearly waiting for me to follow her. There was no other option, I would have to take the hip flask with me. I grabbed my thick shawl, put it around my shoulders, hoping it would divert the attention from the bulk in my dress, and followed the maid downstairs.

The drawing room, although only the second largest in the house, was as grand as one might expect from a townhouse in one of the most fashionable areas of London. Lady Catherine was sitting on a damask sofa, dressed in a dark grey silk gown adorned with exquisite black lace. Her presence was as majestic as ever, although I noticed her back wasn't as straight as it once had been.

"Georgiana, don't act like a scared rabbit, it is not becoming in a lady of your rank. Come in and sit yourself here," she said, patting a petite chair to her left. "Colonel Fitzwilliam has yet to arrive."

My cousin must have left the house shortly after our arrival. I found that rather odd, but didn't ask any questions. Instead, I did as I had been told, and took the seat Lady Catherine had offered. It was very low, and the odd angle made my aunt appear even more imposing. My new perspective also afforded me a view of her lapdog, a black fluff ball barely distinguishable amongst the dark silk of my aunt's skirt. It was a young thing, almost a puppy, and when our eyes met, it raised its ears in my direction, as if in salutation.

"You have grown taller since the last time we met. That's unfortunate. Men tend to prefer petite ladies, with a few notable exceptions."

I wondered if she considered herself to be one of such, for Lady Catherine's height was certainly no trifle, especially for someone of her generation. Her grey gaze continued to observe me carefully, and she seemed otherwise pleased until she saw the laceration on my forehead.

"What is that, may I ask?"

"There was an incident just outside the inn last night."

"What do you mean, an incident?"

I hesitated. The Colonel had asked me not to provide Lady

Catherine with an account of what had happened, so as to spare her any worry. She was weary enough of travelling and roadside inns as it was.

"I bumped my head," I said, unable to think of anything else.

"Clumsiness can be easily avoided with care, attention and grace, Georgiana. Let us pray that it does not leave a scar. Your complexion is your primary blessing in terms of physical beauty. Now, I hope you have been diligent in cultivating your education and accomplishments since our last encounter."

Lady Catherine proceeded to interrogate me about my musical practice, my painting, my dancing, my French, my Italian, and my embroidering. However, she never asked about my brother or his wife. I supposed she had elicited all the information she needed though the servants that had travelled with us.

"I never understood Darcy's obsession with keeping you at Pemberley all these years, out of sight from any society of consequence," she said, stroking her lapdog. "It is foolish to let your youth and bloom go to waste away from potential suitors, especially as you have so little to offer. Your mother's legendary beauty went all to your brother. But you have a pleasant countenance, good teeth and, with some guidance, could develop something akin to elegance."

My cheeks were burning, but Lady Catherine charged ahead.

"I have already written to the Lord Chamberlain's office and asked permission to present you at court. The reply must come at any time now, and the next drawing room is at the end of the coming week, so we only have a few days to get you ready. I have also engaged a team of seamstresses in the preparation of your court dress. They have been working on it for a few weeks now, and they will call early on Monday morning for the fitting. They will also make you some new gowns. You need suitable garments for the remainder of the season, and I have already warned them that they must be exquisite. That old thing you have on you, for example, simply will not do. You must appear as *rich* as possible."

Instinctively, I wrapped the shawl tighter around my shoulders. My aunt must have found my gesture irritating because when she spoke again, her voice was laden with impatience.

"Georgiana, surely you know by now that your appearance cannot possibly get you a husband, and that you have to rely on your settlement to draw male interest. We want *all* eligible bachelors you meet to understand your situation the minute you walk into a room, and heaven knows that with men one often has to make things as plain as possible."

The thought of being presented at court wasn't nearly as terrifying as the idea of entering a room full of strangers to whom I was but thirty-thousand pounds with legs.

My aunt took a sip of her cup of tea and her stern gaze set again on my face. I feared that she could read me like a book, and I grew agitated at the thought of the hip flask hidden in my pocket. What would she think if she saw it? I tried my hardest to keep my composure but my discomfort must have shown, because she narrowed her eyes and intensified her stare.

"Georgiana, is there anything I should know?"

Right at that moment, a carriage stopped just outside. I heard another carriage, and a horse neighed. One of the drivers shouted something in a cockney drawl that I couldn't understand. A minute later, Colonel Fitzwilliam was with us. Lady Catherine, always delighted to have male company, lit up in the presence of her nephew and seemed to forget I was even in the room. Her lips even drew the shadow of a smile as they discussed the health of his immediate family, the weather up north and the London season.

I stifled a yawn. The sky outside had darkened; it had been a long day, and my eyelids were closing. My aunt was never one for subtlety, however. She steadfastly ignored my silent pleas for an early dismissal, and it wasn't until a good hour later that she suggested we went upstairs to get ready for dinner. I was about to ask for permission to retire, eat a cold supper in my room and have an early night when my aunt commanded my cousin's attention.

"I was thinking, Fitzwilliam, that it is lovely to see Georgiana these days. She is the very definition of a well-bred young lady. Such command, such posture."

"I agree, Aunt. She is looking remarkably poised, in spite of the long day she has had."

"Duty above all. She takes after my father's side of the family, you know. Your grandfather, Sir Lewis de Bourgh, was an extraordinary man."

I wasn't sure what my aunt was getting at, so I chose to smile sweetly.

"The family anecdotes certainly suggest so," replied Cousin Fitzwilliam. "Although I dare say that Georgiana isn't that different from her father. I certainly remember the late Mr Darcy as a very duty-bound man."

"Such a pity his son didn't follow in his footsteps."

Lady Catherine's tone was icy cold, as always when speaking about my brother since his marriage to Elizabeth. For once, however, she didn't dwell on the family tensions.

"But really, Colonel, one would never guess Georgiana has been travelling for most of the day. You may be too young to remember, Fitzwilliam, but my sister, although an exquisite creature to look at, was notoriously fickle when it came to fulfilling her social obligations. Fatigue, she would often say. Even as a young girl she had the gravest and most extraordinary imaginary malaises. I always felt sorry for my brother-in-law. He was seen on his own, without the comfort of his wife's presence, far more often than any married man ought to be."

I looked at my cousin with pleading eyes, but the Colonel didn't seem to understand my predicament. Lady Catherine left the lapdog on a silk cushion on the floor and rose from her sofa.

"However, we will continue our conversation later. Dinner will be served shortly."

Crestfallen, I followed her out of the drawing room, but before I reached the stairs my aunt's cold hand closed around my wrist. She leaned in to me.

"Consider this part of your training," she whispered. "I will turn you into the most desirable female in the whole of London this season."

I shuddered.

On Monday morning, the team of seamstresses arrived as early as Lady Catherine had promised. They surrounded me like industrious bees, taking measurements of every part of my body and assenting to everything my aunt said. Lady Catherine supervised the operation like an admiral ordering his officers aboard his ship. She barely asked for my opinion, instructing the women on exactly what they were to provide, in which materials and the sort of finishes and ornaments that were required, but that suited me fine. While I was tugged and pinned and made to extend my arms, I lost myself in my thoughts, wondering about the etching on the hip flask. Was the stranger a Wesley, a Washington, a William? Perhaps a Waldo? Did the date commemorate an engagement, a wedding, a birth? A silver hip flask was expensive. That a man dressed in such simple apparel should own one was odd. He might have borrowed it, of course. The object was well used. He might have bought it cheaply off an owner wanting to get rid of it.

A thought suddenly struck me. Perhaps he had stolen it. Was my saviour a robber? Was that what he had tried to do on the day, jump onto the carriage to appropriate himself of our belongings? I closed my eyes and pictured his concerned gaze when he had found me. No, that had never been his intention, of that I was sure.

Afterwards, Lady Catherine took me to Ludgate Hill. The day was dry but had a tinge of grey all over. From the safety of my aunt's barouche I was able to observe life in the busy London streets, so far removed from Lambton and everything that I had known growing up.

The crowd moved like a giant multicoloured beast. The gentlemen wore elegant top hats and the ladies the most fashionable outfits, but for every decently attired man or woman going about their business, there were at least a handful of wretches lurking in street corners, begging for a coin. And, above all, there were children, many children, some wearing little more than rags that could not possibly protect them from the still cold temperatures of late winter.

My heart swelled at the sight of three young boys, one of them barely out of babyhood, begging in a street corner. The oldest one, who could not be more than six or seven, had a sailor hat on. They must be war orphans. With their bare feet, their chapped skin red and raw, they seemed much more miserable than the Pemberley poor I had become accustomed to visiting under Elizabeth's guidance. The old servants who lived in the cottages at the end of the state, the sick workers who were no longer able to feed their families, the widows who had to rely on charity to raise their young, they all represented a sort of genteel poverty, far removed from the desperate destitution of city beggars.

A carriage in front of us abruptly stopped, and the barouche came to a halt right next to where the three children were standing.

The boy with the hat immediately took note of the shiny doors and the livery of Lady Catherine's carriage, and made a gesture to the middle child. In response, his brother took the toddler by the hand and dragged him in our direction. Encouraged by his sibling, the little one stretched his hand out to me, and I saw his clouded eyes. He was blind.

I had the urge to stop the carriage, to send for Jones and get her to bring me all the coins I kept in the purse by my bedside table. I wanted to give the unfortunate children warm clothes, plenty of food and the assurance that they would never have to beg again, but a single look from my aunt silenced me. Under her mute command, I tore my gaze away from the window, ashamed at my lack of gumption.

I was still shaking when the coachman dropped us off right outside the jewellers that my aunt had chosen as purveyors of the diamond-encrusted bandeau that was to complete my headdress. The piece was ostentatious and rather heavy, but my aunt was adamant that there was no alternative possible for my presentation, such were the strict rules surrounding court attire. She made me try it on. As well as uncomfortable and not particularly flattering, the bandeau seemed to me incongruous and detached from reality, a leftover from past times, and wearing it I felt like a little girl playing with her mother's belongings.

Before we left the shop, Lady Catherine insisted I bought some more jewellery.

"There is *nothing* like big stones to enhance your

appearance, my dear."

I looked at all the items on display and chose a lovely gold cross with a single diamond at its centre and an exquisitely chain of tiny pearls. My aunt's eyes narrowed.

"Your future husband shall be delighted with your tastes, Georgiana," she said, her lips pursing. "What man wouldn't wish for a wife with thirty-thousand pounds who spends like a shopkeeper's mistress?"

I coloured deeply.

"But aunt, this is what I like."

"Nonsense. We will have a look at the brooch over there," Lady Catherine commanded the jeweller, pointing towards a brooch in the main display.

With affected reverence, the man did as he was told and placed the piece on a velvet tray in front of us. The item in question was as big as the palm of my hand and had an intricate design depicting a butterfly and a flower. The main motives were studded with gold, opal and pearls, and two sapphires and two rubies the size of my thumbnails adorned the insect's wings. It would appear that the sole purpose of its maker had been to cram in as many precious stones in a single piece as possible.

"This is much more suitable," said my aunt, her voice brimming with approval.

"But I don't have any dresses in those colours. It doesn't really go with my aqua gown, it's too pale. Or my pink one."

"Georgiana, you cannot possibly have forgotten. You are

getting new ones! We will take it," said Lady Catherine turning to the jeweller.

With a huge grin, the jeweller assured us that he would make the necessary arrangements to deliver both pieces to Grosvenor Square at the earliest convenience.

When we left the store, I felt faintly sick at the outcome of my shopping expedition. Purchasing such hideous items at such prices was bad enough. Not having had the decency to give the waifs in the street corner a couple of coins was infinitely worse.

Chapter 7

At the end of my third full day in London, Mr and Mrs Collins joined us for dinner at my aunt's Grosvenor Square residence. I had met Mr Collins, the clergyman at the Hunsford parsonage near Rosings Park, on a previous occasion many years before. He was a pompous little man with no sense of humour or ridicule and an obsequiousness that rather irritated me. Our encounter took place before he married, so I was intrigued at the prospect of making Mrs Collins' acquaintance, on account of her having been an intimate friend of Elizabeth's for many years. However, Mrs Collins turned out to be disappointingly discreet and she said little during our conversation, although enough to make it abundantly clear that she was much more sensible than her husband.

As soon as we sat down at the table in the small dining room,

Mr Collins stood up and cleared his throat.

"Lady Catherine de Bourgh," he said in an affected voice, "It is such a great honour that you should welcome us, your humble servants, to your magnificent London residence. I was just saying to Mrs Collins the other night, I do wonder how Lady Catherine de Bourgh is doing, and whether she will have noticed our card. I am so relieved to see you looking so remarkably well, madam. If I may say so, that colour particularly suits your complexion."

"You may not say so, Mr Collins, mainly because my complexion is far from what it used to be. But you may pay a similar compliment to my niece."

"Miss Darcy, the shade you are wearing brings out the perfect paleness of your skin, if I may say so as a married man."

"Never apologise for being a married man, Mr Collins, especially not for having such a dutiful and obliging wife," roared my aunt. "If only all married men were like you."

"My dear Lady Catherine, am I right in thinking you are still sourly disappointed in one of our kin? I very much hope that my cousin has been doing her best to regain your favour."

"Your cousin is her usual insolent self, and my nephew continues to be under her spell."

I knew that my aunt never had any affection for Elizabeth, but to hear her debase her name outside of the strict family circle, with no regard for my feelings or the Darcy name, was most unpleasant. Alarmed, I searched my cousin's eyes, but he seemed to be absent in everything but his physical presence.

My aunt hadn't finished.

"What is worse, her family is at Pemberley more than ever before. Georgiana has been quite turned out of her own home on account of their latest visit. It breaks my heart to think of that noble house being polluted by their vulgar manners and tedious talk, but even more so to see it become a haven to those who indulge in the most *unacceptable* of behaviours."

I wondered what she meant by that. Surely, the Bennets were harmless enough?

"Do not say, Lady Catherine! I shudder to think what they must have done to offend you so," replied Mr Collins with glee.

My aunt looked at him conspiratorially and lowered her voice.

"My maid has it on good authority that the youngest sister, the one who infamously eloped with my late brother-in-law's steward's son, is still welcome at Pemberley. That the Bennet family circle should continue to receive her as if nothing had happened shows a shocking lack of delicacy. But that her presence should also be welcome in what used to be a bastion of exquisite manners and impeccable morals simply has no words."

Lady Catherine's vitriol brought Colonel Fitzwilliam back to reality.

"May I remind you that Mr and Mrs Wickham are now married, Lady Catherine?"

"Heaven knows why. The young man was a bright child, but your uncle was too soft on him. For a time I thought he would make the most of the undue privileges he had received, acquire presence, go into the law and marry a superior, someone with money. He certainly had the looks, the charm and the polish to aim for a change in situation. I was very surprised when he didn't, and I'm not often surprised. Regardless, that Mrs Wickham should be received at Pemberley is truly scandalous."

"Your words are harsh, Lady Catherine," intervened my cousin, alarmed at the turn the conversation was taking.

"Nonsense! In every single elopement, whether it succeeds or not, the blame is always on the female, for a decorous woman would never consent to such dishonourable plans. If anything, her relatives should also be seen as responsible, for she would have necessarily been subject to lack of attentive vigilance, which as everyone knows can fuel disreputable behaviour in even the most virtuous girls. A young woman who dares to enter matrimony without the knowledge or approval of her parents or guardians should *never* be allowed into polite society again."

The spoon fell off my fingers as if they were made out of warm butter, and it clanked against the porcelain of the bowl in front of me. Colonel Fitzwilliam glanced in my direction with concern.

"The soup is delicious, Lady Catherine. Is Cook new?" he asked, in a debonair voice.

But my aunt wasn't having any of it.

"You now understand why I have come to believe that Darcy's home is not a suitable place for Georgiana anymore. She is at such a delicate age."

Mr Collins, who had sat through my aunt's criticisms without saying a word and had such mirth in his eyes it was evident he had been enjoying them, intervened with his usual servility.

"Lady Catherine, I beg you, say no more. I fully recognise and appreciate the gravity of your predicament, and I pray that your pious heart will find the necessary strength to overcome the worries brought upon you by your ungrateful nephew and niece-in-law."

Then, to my surprise, Mr Collins turned to me.

"Miss Darcy, allow me to remind you that you are the most fortunate young woman in England. Your aunt's concern for you is such that she has forced herself to forsake the natural desire for withdrawal and prayer that comes after the loss of a child to attend to your needs. You are blessed to have her as your guide in London."

I nodded. It was sad that cousin Anne's tragic demise should be mentioned at all, but at least we had moved on from talking about the eternal damnation that elopements brought to young ladies.

Mr Collins was right in that Lady Catherine had been unusually quiet for a good three of years after her daughter's death. At the time she wasn't on the best of terms with Fitzwilliam, and things at Pemberley were particularly busy with the arrival of little Will. I felt guilty. Perhaps I should have spent more time with my aunt at Rosings. It wasn't the most appealing of prospects, but it was my duty towards an older relative. I feared I had been too self-absorbed.

Lady Catherine was not entirely displeased with the way the conversation was going.

"Mr Collins, were you more observant, you would have noticed that Georgiana is perfectly aware of the extraordinariness of the situation. Most pressingly, she only has this season to find a husband."

My ears perked up. I knew that Lady Catherine was determined to marry me, ideally before the end of the summer, but it had never crossed my mind that her mission had a particular deadline.

"I thought Miss Darcy was but twenty," said Mrs Collins with surprise.

"She will not be for long now, Mr Collins, and no female in my family has ever married past their twenty-first year. It is a truth universally acknowledged that a woman over that age has lost her bloom, and it is very likely that she will remain a spinster forever."

Silence fell around the table. Mrs Collins coloured deeply, and her husband patted her hand.

"Of course, this applies mostly to our superiors, my dear Mrs Collins," he muttered in a tone loud enough for everyone to hear.

"Oh, Mr Collins, your wife is the exception to the rule," Lady Catherine added with no remorse in her voice. "But you and I know how she was always your second choice, and that the lady you originally intended was indeed not yet twenty. Imagine, however, if you had ended up marrying *her*."

My aunt let out a strange laugh. Mr Collins chuckled nervously; Mrs Collins' knuckles were white.

I didn't understand. Who had Mr Collins wanted to marry? Judging by my aunt's comments, he had been turned down by a female she didn't favour.

Elizabeth?

Impossible. The notion was grotesque. Still, Mr Collins and Elizabeth were cousins, and he was set to inherit Longbourn, the Bennet family estate, which was subject to an entail. There might have been a point in the past when the match was considered very desirable. I had to stifle a giggle.

During the rest of the meal, the conversation was kept safely away from any sensitive topics by my diligent cousin. The last course was being served when Mr Collins circumspectly raised the topic of my marriage again. Lady Catherine had been speaking about her many seasons in the capital back in the day when her father, the late Earl Fitzwilliam, was a peer.

"Believe me, the entertainment on offer during the London season used to be the best in the world. Parties were always opulent and dignified affairs, with the most exquisite musicians, the most talented dancers and incredibly imaginative food and drink concoctions. The fashion, too, was much more becoming to both males and females. Everyone looks so common these days. However, Georgiana must be seen, so I will have to make sacrifices and go out in society if she is to marry well."

Mr Collins turned towards me with the look of a hunter picking a puppy out of its mother's litter.

"I have no doubt that Miss Darcy will be received with much admiration. Have you any candidates in mind for her, Lady Catherine?"

I felt affronted at Mr Collins' question and the inherent expectation it contained. My aunt certainly wasn't going to discuss my prospects in front of her vicar and his wife.

How wrong I was.

Lady Catherine smacked her lips.

"I have great designs for Georgiana. I believe she could easily attract the attention of gentlemen of a certain stature."

Mr Collins almost applauded her.

"Someone titled! Indeed, what a *perfect* idea, Lady Catherine. Your niece has a generous settlement, and the number of noble families that find themselves in want of prosperous alliances to enhance their inherited estates seems to be increasing by the day. Moreover, I have always said to Mrs Collins that your niece has exceptional posture, just what is required in aristocratic circles."

I believed I cared little about what a man like Mr Collins thought of me, but his words stung. The fact that, when it came to my looks, even a natural flatterer of his statue could praise little other than my posture was disheartening.

By the time Mr and Mrs Collins left, I had a splitting headache, a knot in my stomach and the overwhelming desire to hide in my room for the rest of my London stay. I was also astonished that a woman as apparently judicious as Mrs Collins should have married someone like Mr Collins. But before I was able to retire for bed, my cousin brought up the subject of my suitors again.

"With all due respect, Lady Catherine, although Georgiana's settlement is indeed very large, it may not be sufficient for the purposes of marrying an aristocrat."

My aunt dismissed his objections with a hand gesture.

"Nonsense. I may as well tell you now. I have decided that, considering that my dear Anne is no longer with us, Georgiana will be the heiress of Rosings Park."

Hearing those words was like being slapped on both ears at the same time. Rosings Park. I was going to be an extraordinarily rich woman. Certainly, much more than I ever imagined, or even cared. I already had more than I would ever need. I felt faint. My aunt's plans would make my fortune much harder to bear, for I had no doubt that Lady Catherine's generosity came attached with expectations of the highest order.

My cousin was clearly as shocked as I was.

"Don't look at me like that, Fitzwilliam," Lady Catherine snapped. "You will get a very generous settlement from me, which heaven knows you need. I know of your weaknesses, of course, I do. But think about Georgiana. When the knowledge emerges that she will receive the bulk of the de Bourgh's inheritance, the highest-ranking men in town will be interested in her. We simply have to make sure she is seen, and that she looks magnificent in every single outing."

Lady Catherine called her lapdog, put it on her lap and gave the pet a biscuit.

"This reminds me, Georgiana," she said turning to me, "has your new brooch been delivered yet?"

Colonel Fitzwilliam looked at me with surprise.

"Have you been shopping for new jewellery, Georgiana? Darcy told me that your mother left you a rather extensive collection."

"Oh, Fitzwilliam, how little you understand women!" barked Lady Catherine in his direction. "No wonder you are not married yet. A few of my sister's gems are passable, but most of the settings look very old-fashioned and it is about time Georgiana started buying pieces to suit her own taste. Next week we will go back to the jewellers and have some of her mother's things remodelled into more current styles, so she can at least get some wear out of them. She could do with some more pearl strings. Georgiana, you should also ask your brother to send the rest of them, or at least as many of them as you can convince him to part with. Darcy can be ridiculously sentimental sometimes."

I thought of Mama's gems, how carefully they had been stored all these years and the reverence with which my brother showed them to me on particular occasions. Each piece had its own story. The emerald ring Mama received from my father when she gave him the heir he so desired; the thick, solid gold bracelet with exotic carvings that my great-grandfather brought back for my great-grandmother from a heroic journey to the East; the pearl and ruby necklace that His Majesty Charles II gifted a beautiful great-great-aunt who, rumour had it, had become his mistress. Fitzwilliam would never consent to their desecration.

The Colonel, well aware of this, was watching me with intent. However, disagreeing with Lady Catherine when my future happiness so depended on her favour was unthinkable. My aunt despised disobedience, particularly in young females. Upon realising that I would not object to Lady Catherine's plans, Colonel Fitzwilliam spoke somewhat abruptly.

"Lady Catherine, Georgiana may find that she needs her brother's approval before resetting her mother's jewels."

"Nonsense. The gems are hers by birthright."

"Not all of them. There is also Mrs Darcy."

At the mention of Elizabeth, Lady Catherine roared like a wounded lioness.

"I will not have that woman tell my niece what to do. She has harmed her prospects badly enough by keeping her locked up and under her watch all this time."

I was shocked at my aunt's words. That wasn't at all my experience of the time I had spent with my brother and his wife at Pemberley. It had been a happy time, only occasionally tarnished by my melancholy at the memory of Wickham.

My cousin was livid, but his manners never wavered.

"Lady Catherine," he said with perfect command, "Seeing

that you do not intend to do the same now Georgiana is staying with you, I assume that you will allow her to visit Mr and Mrs Gardiner, Miss Bennet and Miss Catherine Bennet."

My aunt looked at him with distaste.

"Colonel, I object to you making such a suggestion."

The Colonel didn't lose his cool.

"The Gardiners and the Misses Bennet are all close relations of Georgiana's on account of her brother's marriage. And I must say, I think very highly of Mrs Gardiner. She is an elegant, highly respectable woman who is exerting an excellent influence on her younger charges. Moreover, Georgiana is well acquainted with the Gardiners through their visits to Pemberley. She has also met Mrs Darcy's sisters, who are approximately her age, on several occasions. Surely, if she does not see them in London, her decision will quickly become the subject of malicious gossip."

Lady Catherine was silent for a few minutes.

"I suppose it would be improper for Georgiana to avoid their company while she is in town," she finally said, "but I cannot abide the thought of receiving them at Grosvenor Square."

I felt compelled to make myself heard. After all, the discussion was about my social circle.

"Dear Aunt, perhaps I could invite them to join me on a trip in your barouche if you are so kind as to acquiesce," I said in a thin voice.

Lady Catherine seemed satisfied with my idea. After agreeing that I would send them a note arranging an encounter outside of the house, so my aunt didn't have to see them, there was no further comment on the matter.

Chapter 8

The following days were a flurry of more dress fittings and tedious beauty treatments that Jones applied to my skin with the veneration that one may save for one's evening prayers. I was often tempted to tell her that no amount of attention would be able to transform me into a society beauty overnight, but she laboured with such belief that I had no option but to keep quiet. My wound was healing quickly, just as the stranger had promised. I still had the urge to find him, properly thank him for his assistance on that fateful day and return to him the hip flask that was hidden at the bottom of one my trunks. I had polished the dull metal with a cloth, and it now gleamed, the scratches barely visible, just the dents telling the world about its temerarious existence. I had to give it back to its rightful owner, but I didn't know where to begin.

The day of my court appearance finally arrived. I dressed

with the help of Cosette, my aunt's French maid, because Lady Catherine deemed Jones to be unsuitable for such a complex task and dismissed her for the day, much to the girl's chagrin. As was to be expected, the finished costume was incredibly elaborate. It had a bodice in the softest white velvet with a superb crisscrossing of silver ropes and tassels and a delicate silver border at the bottom. The white satin skirt and long train were delicately embroidered, showing an intricate display of leaves, flowers and feathers which represented Pemberley, the Darcy family estate. I wondered how the seamstresses had managed to create a thing of such beauty in so little time, but I expected the answer to be in the high price paid for the outfit.

Cosette took her time, carefully and systematically pinning, buttoning and lacing the many openings of the dress while I tried to keep as still as possible. I had been instructed not to eat or drink anything, so as to avoid bodily urgencies once at St James, and under the stiff and heavy costume I could feel my stomach protesting at the lack of breakfast that morning.

Cosette's brown eyes were as stern as my aunt's.

"Please try to relax, madam. I cannot work properly if you move all the time," she mumbled in a thick accent as she was adjusting the white ostrich feathers in the heavy diamond bandeau placed on my head.

After some fumbling, the last feather went into the headpiece. I looked at my reflection in the mirror and barely recognised the young woman looking back at me. Cosette had deftly applied some discreet ointments to my face, and as a result, my skin seemed to light up from the inside. I instinctively checked my hairline: the small scar was barely visible. It was quickly fading, just as my remembrance of the features of my saviour, which was as well. His threadbare coat was a world away from my court dress.

A few minutes later the door opened and Lady Catherine entered the room. She appraised me with narrow eyes, then slowly nodded.

"Excellent job, Cosette. Georgiana, may I see your curtsey?"

I gulped. I had practised my deep curtsey uncountable times in the last week, always with the hoops around my waist, but never in full dress or wearing the bandeau. Slowly, I took hold of my wide skirt and bent my head forward, keeping my neck straight, as if an invisible puppeteer was pulling my feathered crown in his direction. Then, I started to bend my knees outward, again making sure that my back remained as rigid as a plank. When my knees were like twigs about to break, I stopped and kept my body as still as my legs would allow.

I waited for Lady Catherine to signal for me to come out of the position. My legs were burning and my knees started to shake, but my aunt remained silent. The tension was beginning to make my whole body tremble. I kept it as much as I could under control, silently begging for the torture to end. Finally, a light tap on my shoulder with a fan. Lady Catherine was giving me permission to straighten my legs. Slowly, I started to do so. Then I heard Colette gasp.

Through the corner of my eye, I saw one of the white feathers come undone and fall to the floor like an autumnal leaf. Lady Catherine's approving nods turned into a mask of distaste. She looked at her maid with those cold, calculating eyes of hers.

"Cosette, this is unacceptable," she said with a menacing air. "If you make a fool of my niece, you shall be making a fool her sponsor. And nobody makes a fool of Lady Catherine de Bourgh. Do you understand?"

The maid was distraught, tears streaming down her cheeks, but she nodded profusely and gave her desperate assurances that all would be fixed in time for the presentation. An hour later, after Cosette had thoroughly inspected all the feathers, ribbons and other accessories in my outfit to ensure they were all safely attached, I was finally placed in my aunt's barouche, and we left in the direction of St James.

* * *

We got to the palace in due course, but had to wait for a long time, and standing, alas. I had the suspicion that titled young ladies were given precedence; for once, my wealth and social status didn't have the least importance.

The drawing room at St James was spacious and imposing, its ceilings high and beautifully ornate. The large arched windows, dressed with heavy velvet curtains, allowed much light into the space, which had richly lined walls, covered with gilded-framed paintings depicting portraits of royalty and nobility and the odd pastoral scene. Courtiers were everywhere, all of them in elaborate and vibrant dress, colourful like a colony of butterflies. The air was thick with sweat and the perfumes of exotic flowers and spices intended to mask bodily odours. I had expected the room to be solemnly silent, but I couldn't have been further from the truth: there was a constant buzz in the background, to the point that one might think that an army of bees had entered through one of the garden windows.

I felt faintly sick. The bandeau, heavier by the minute, was tight around my temples, as if a giant was steadily pressing my skull with his mighty hands. My nerves and the tight gown had quelled the ravenous hunger I was feeling before leaving Grosvenor Square, but my mouth was dry and sticky. What if the Queen addressed me and I couldn't answer?

The Lord Chamberlain finally announced me, and my aunt gave me one of her commanding looks. I swallowed hard and advanced towards the Queen. She was sitting in perfect stillness, like an ancient sculpture, her frail body magnificently attired with a formal court dress in embroidered gold and silver cloth. She was not a handsome woman like my aunt, who at her age still kept a faint trace of the delicate features of her youth, but her bearing was distinctively regal, and she had an air of natural authority.

The Queen acknowledged my presence with the faintest of nods. As if on cue, I began my curtsey, lowering myself down and praying that the ostrich feathers would stay firmly in their place. My legs, tired from standing for hours, attempted to rebel, but I persisted, and curtseyed in front of the Queen in a single graceful movement. I smiled inwardly; my aunt would be proud. I slowly rose up again, and my eyes met the Queen's. She looked at me with a jaded expression and extended her hand to be kissed.

"Do you like horses?" she asked me, unexpectedly.

We had excellent stables at Pemberley, full of mounts of the best breeds, beautiful animals that I enjoyed riding in the lush green of the estate. However, upon hearing the Queen's question, a very particular memory hit me: the distinctive smell of horse, tobacco and wet wool of the stranger I had encountered at the inn. I blushed.

"I do, ma'am. Very much."

She turned to the crowd, and with a hand wave, she dismissed me.

I had almost finished. I bent again for another deep curtsey. Long neck, straight back, bent knees. Down, down, then stop. Confident, I rose again. Then, out of nowhere, I lost my balance. It was just a split second, and I quickly gained my composure again. I don't think the Queen noticed; her attention had wandered elsewhere. But I was certain that Lady Catherine would reprimand me as soon as we got back to the house. I slowly walked backwards out of the Queen's presence, my self-assurance dented, praying that I would not trip over my train or any unforeseen obstacles.

When I joined Lady Catherine, she did not say a word, but her seething discontent was apparent in the way she grabbed my arm and started to drag me towards the door. I resigned myself to the reprimand that no doubt would come as soon as we were seated in her carriage, but as we moved through the room, she went stiff, then nodded, and slowly but surely changed her course towards one of the windows.

A carefully coiffed gentleman of a certain age in full ceremonial dress of richly embroidered coat and breeches ceremoniously greeted my aunt, and then addressed her warmly.

"Lady Catherine de Bourgh, I cannot believe my eyes! It is so wonderful to see you at court."

"Lord Elliot, it is a pleasure to be here again."

My aunt kept her usual dignified bearing, but I knew her well enough to realise that she was as delighted to be recognised at St James as a milkmaid the first time the farmer's son notices her. I let out a sigh of relief, hoping the encounter would radically transform her mood for the rest of the day.

Lady Catherine began to converse amicably with Lord Elliot. From their dialogue, it transpired that the families were acquainted on account of the Elliots being relatives of Lady Dalrymple, a childhood friend of my aunt's. Lord Elliot had not seen Lady Catherine for years, and he immediately offered his condolences on Cousin Anne's passing. His manners were elegant in the extreme, his solicitude to my aunt very apparent, and he was, or rather had been, a handsome man. I wondered whether he had been one of the candidates Lady Catherine had considered as a prospective son-in-law after Cousin Anne's presumed engagement to my brother dissolved. I made a mental note to ask Jones upon returning to Grosvenor Square; she would know.

The conversation then moved on to me.

"I must congratulate you on the presentation of your niece, Lady Catherine. She is rather delightful."

Lord Elliot's gaze fell on my body, and he unashamedly appraised my person like a patron at a tobacconist might assess a valuable gem-encrusted snuff box. Then, he smacked his lips in approval, and gave me what appeared like a much-rehearsed smile. I lowered my eyes, passing off my revulsion as maiden modesty.

"Yes, she is very delightful, and no doubt very accomplished as well. Is she staying with you at Grosvenor Square?"

"She is, Lord Elliot, and she will be for the remainder of the season."

"Very well. I imagine my cousins the Dalrymples will be expecting your presence at Hanover Square for their upcoming *soirée*. Lady Dalrymple will no doubt be anxious to see you. I know fully well how much she esteems you."

"Indeed, Lord Elliot. We have received Lady Dalrymple's invitation, and I am looking forward to introducing Georgiana to her next Tuesday."

"And I look forward to continuing our conversation, Lady Catherine, as well as deepening my acquaintance with your charming niece."

Lord Elliot gave us an elegant bow in way of farewell.

Shortly afterwards we were back in the barouche, my aunt deep in thought. I expected her to mention my curtseying blunder, but the encounter with Lord Elliot had caused her attention to direct itself elsewhere, and I couldn't but be grateful to Lord Elliot for having spared me grief.

* * *

Colonel Fitzwilliam joined us for dinner that night. In spite of his recent differences with Lady Catherine, he seemed his usual charming self. Likewise, my aunt did not allude to their disagreement. I suspected that, with my brother banished from Lady Catherine's affections due to his choice of wife, the Colonel had readily become my aunt's favourite nephew.

The first thing the Colonel expressed was his regret at not having seen me before I set off for my presentation at St James.

"If only I could have convinced Mr Marshall to amend our plans, but it was impossible. Georgiana in full court attire must have been quite a beautiful sight. But pray, tell me, how did the ceremony go?"

Lady Catherine, who was in excellent spirits, did not allow the memory of my gaffe to spoil her delight.

"It was wonderful to be at court after such a long time and to find that one still has acquaintances in the most exclusive of social circles in the country," she said, her voice brimming with pleasure.

"We encountered Lord Elliot, a cousin of the late Lord Dalrymple. Both families were estranged for a while, but they appear to be on excellent terms again. I find it odd that Lord Elliot has not yet remarried. He is still young enough to produce a male heir."

I considered my aunt's words for a few moments. Lord Elliot retained some of the features that must have marked him as very good-looking in his youth, but he was most certainly in the mature years of his life, and certainly past his prime. Whether he could father children was no given, but I supposed that for dozens of women he represented a very desirable match.

"It may have been a wonderfully exciting day, but I fear that it may have affected Georgiana's nerves," the Colonel said, putting his fork on the silver plate. "She looks terribly pale and hasn't eaten but a morsel of what has been put in front of her."

I guiltily thought of the feast of bread, cold meats and cheese I had eaten upon arriving at Grosvenor Square. The hours of standing on an empty stomach at St James Palace had left me ravenous, and the food, not my health, was to blame for my lack of appetite. But before I could explain myself, my aunt intervened. Her good mood had disappeared like the sun behind a stormy cloud.

"Georgiana must become accustomed to being in public and acquire the habit of conversation. You and I know that her days in Pemberley are numbered. She will soon have a home to call her own, and if everything goes according to my designs, her new responsibilities will include many social engagements at the highest level."

Colonel Fitzwilliam smiled.

"Dear Lady Catherine, you speak as if Georgiana were engaged, but unless you have been secretly meeting up with eligible bachelors under the pretence of shopping for ribbons, I don't think she is much closer to marriage than she was when we left Pemberley."

"Oh, but she is. She was seen at court today, and she will be seen much more in what remains of the season. Dinners, balls, concerts, assemblies – I have it all planned. On Tuesday, my old friend Lady Dalrymple is hosting a small party with the most elegant and select group of guests. It will be an excellent first event for Georgiana. I have it on good word that there will be one or two extremely eligible single men in the party."

Lady Catherine narrowed her eyes and raised her eyebrows, as if she could picture the possibilities of the gathering. I pondered my aunt's words, and secretly hoped that Lord Elliot was not one of the single men she was contemplating as potential suitors for my hand.

"Lady Darlymple has also invited us to a ball on the following Friday, which will be a much grander affair. Colonel, you will accompany us on both occasions, will you not? Lady Dalrymple is terribly eager to check for herself if you look like your father. You will remember that she met him many years ago."

My cousin smiled at her curtly.

"If you excuse me, Lady Catherine, I am otherwise engaged

on Tuesday night. I arranged several months ago to meet with some old officers from my battalion. Many of them are coming from afar, so I have no option to reschedule it. However, it will be my pleasure to escort you to the ball on Friday."

Lady Catherine reluctantly accepted the Colonel's excuse, and with that particular course of events agreed upon, we all retired to our rooms. I, for one, was glad to have an early night.

Chapter 9

The interior of Lady Dalrymple's Hanover Square residence was as grand as the exterior. Lady Catherine and I went up the long marble staircase, flanked by large family portraits of people long dead, all with similarly haughty expressions, and were ushered into the main drawing room. Lady Dalrymple was sitting on a throne-like chair, dressed in the most traditional fashion.

My aunt went to her, and I followed.

"Lady Dalrymple, it is a great pleasure to see you. May I introduce my niece, Miss Darcy? She's my late sister's daughter. I am sure you will see the resemblance, although it has been a long time since we played together in our childhood. Georgiana was so eager to meet you. I have explained to her how kind you were to Lady Anne, and how you let her play with your favourite doll."

Lady Dalrymple stared at me with empty eyes, a rigid smile

on her aged face, then gave me a sort of side nod. I quickly lowered my gaze and curtseyed. I was then introduced to Lady Dalrymple's only daughter, Miss Carteret, who was rather plain and awkward, in spite of her beautiful clothes and expensive jewellery. Where her mother was vacuously charming and indifferent, Miss Carteret came across as nervous, like a sparrow suspecting a bird of prey. Next to her, I felt positively elegant, even pretty.

Under my aunt's severe gaze I tried to engage in polite conversation with Miss Carteret, but she was barely civil and just gave me the shortest of answers. She kept glancing now and again towards the magnificent golden clock on the mantelpiece.

Then, the main door opened, and I saw anticipation in Miss Carteret's expression, as if her life depended on whoever came in now.

Lord Elliot and a handsome lady with an elegant air entered the room. Both were dressed very fashionably and shared a strong family resemblance. They approached us and, after the customary greetings, the lady was introduced to me as Miss Elliot, Lord Elliot's daughter.

Addressing her, Lord Elliot nodded in my direction.

"Dear Elizabeth, is Miss Darcy not a most charming young lady?"

I blushed.

"She is indeed, Papa."

"Miss Darcy, do you play the pianoforte?"

"I do, sir."

"Wonderful. The tinkling of the ivories after dinner can be so enchanting. I do hope you will indulge us later on. My daughter can play only tolerably well, but of course, she has many other charms."

"I am sure she does, Lord Elliot," said my aunt with a frozen smile.

Lord Elliot did not appear to notice my aunt's remark, and after some consideration, he spoke again.

"Lady Catherine, I predict that Miss Darcy will have no trouble finding suitors," he declared with the rational approach other men might reserve for a business transaction. "She will come with a handsome settlement, of course. Under such conditions, even I might be tempted!" he chuckled with glee.

My aunt appeared slightly disconcerted, but before she could respond, the door open again and Miss Carteret's face lit up. This time, a party of three came in: it consisted of a couple, the arm of the lady wrapped around that of her partner, followed by a very tall and broad gentleman. Miss Carteret looked crestfallen, but everyone else's gaze immediately fell on the pair.

The first gentleman, evidently a military man of some description, was exceptionally handsome. His lady, slight and rather pretty in an unassuming sort of way, appeared as dainty and fragile as a meadow flower next to him. Their friend stood in the background, perhaps aware of the interest generated by the couple.

Lady Catherine observed them with narrowing eyes.

"What a fine man. She is not much to look at, but I am certain I have never met *him* before. I have an excellent memory, Lord Elliot. I must ask your cousin, Lady Dalrymple, to introduce me."

"I will be delighted to do the honours, Madam. They are no other than my second daughter Anne and her husband, Captain Wentworth. They have not been married a year. The man behind them is a friend of his, a captain or other. Captain Wentworth is most elegant, is he not?" added Lord Elliot with evident satisfaction.

For once, Lady Catherine reddened, but Lord Elliot didn't seem particularly bothered by my aunt's *faux pas*. He waved to the newcomers, and they made their way towards us.

The Wentworths were an enchanting couple. Captain Wentworth had the boldness and confidence of someone who has been through the worst and has come back intact. His wife had a gentle countenance and seemed somehow timid, although for obvious reasons I was in no position to berate her reserve. The second gentleman, a Captain Price, was pleasant enough. I detected a hint of surprise in his eyes when we were introduced, as if he recognised me. He certainly looked familiar, but I couldn't quite place him.

There was much talking about the weather, London society and the situations of some common acquaintances. Throughout the conversation I was relieved to notice that Lord Elliot seemed much more interested in pleasing and attending to Lady Dalrymple and

Miss Carteret than in getting to know me. Perhaps he was not the bachelor my aunt had in mind for me, after all. Jones had informed me that Lady Catherine had indeed considered Lord Elliot as a suitor to Anne before her health took a turn for the worse, but that had been some years prior, and at the time my cousin was much older than me. I very much hoped my aunt's opinions had changed since.

Some minutes later, I noticed Captain Price's gaze on mine, and when I had the chance, I discreetly addressed him.

"Captain Price, may I ask you if we are acquainted? I have the feeling that we have met before."

He gave me a broad smile.

"If you mean whether we have been formally introduced, I can categorically say that this isn't the case," he said, his blue eyes dancing.

Captain Price was not as handsome as Captain Wentworth, but he had an agreeable countenance and was taller than me, something I wasn't used to. I found myself attracted to his powerful presence, but before either of us could say anything else, the footman announced the arrival of another guest.

"Don Cosimo Giovanni Ludovico, Prince of Rasiglia and Ponziano."

The man who entered the room had the nose of a Roman statue, the poise of a cat and the most perfectly aligned teeth I had ever seen. He was wearing a daring mauve jacket and a delicate lace cravat, and his shiny black hair was arranged in the continental manner. Miss Carteret was all smiles now, her cheeks flushed with colour.

There was a flurry of interactions, greetings, small talk. Then the introductions started, and all of a sudden Don Cosimo was in front of me. He had a strong jaw and a half smile on his handsome face, but all I could see were his eyes. Other than their dazzling green colour, their shape, the long eyelashes, the gentle brow, all screamed Wickham. It was as if a rug had been pulled from under my feet. I curtseyed, then he was gone. I looked up and saw Captain Price observing me in silence, an impenetrable expression on his face.

We made our way to the magnificently opulent dining room and I was seated next to Captain Wentworth, who appeared to be experienced in the art of making conversation. I inwardly sighed with relief; at least maintaining small talk with him wouldn't feel taxing, unlike my earlier attempts with Miss Carteret. To my left, I could glimpse Don Cosimo. His perfectly drawn features were entirely focused on Miss Carteret, on his left-hand side. Across from me, Lord Elliot played a complicated game of tennis, dividing his attention equally between Lady Dalrymple and my aunt, and appeared to have completely forgotten about my existence.

The servants brought in the soup, and the meal began. Captain Price discreetly glanced in my direction every so often, but at the same time seemed to avoid my gaze. His flicker of recognition was gnawing at me, and I must have frowned.

"You seemed concerned about something, Miss Darcy," said Captain Wentworth.

"Not quite, sir. I was just wondering where I might have met your friend, Captain Price. I am convinced we are somehow acquainted, as unlikely as that is. You see, I have not been in society much. Pray, tell me, is he originally from Derbyshire?"

"Derbyshire, you say? An unlikely home for a sailor if I ever heard of one. No, Miss Darcy, he's from Portsmouth. His mother was a Bertram, as in the Bertrams of Mansfield Park. Lord Bertram is his uncle. Perhaps you are acquainted with the family?"

I shook my head. The Bertram name didn't mean much to me.

"Captain Price is an excellent man, and one of the bravest sailors I've ever had the pleasure to work with. He was a second lieutenant at the *Laconia* for a while and then became the first lieutenant at the *Leonidas* under Captain Harvey. Alas, his luck turned sour then."

"How so, Captain Wentworth?"

A shadow darkened his noble features.

"Captain Harvey was a disgrace to the profession. He was a man of barely any morals, and no sense of duty whatsoever, who only made it to captain on account of a very wealthy relative who was happy to sponsor his promotions in the Navy so as to keep him away from land. He relied on his first lieutenant for everything, and Price was captain in all but name. Captain Harvey would often lock himself up in his quarters and drink himself to sleep, with no regard for those under his command. On one such occasion at the peak of the war, Captain Price behaved most courageously in a crucial clash that claimed many of our countrymen's lives. His eye for the battle and unwavering bravery not only saved those on the *Leonidas*, but also drove the ship to victory. However, Captain Harvey took all the credit, and with it, the lion's share of a prize that was justly not his."

"That is appalling!"

"Lieutenant Price was made Captain, but these are bad times for getting on, and as a result his fortune is much less than it ought to be, with little prospect of change ahead. A most unfortunate affair, madam, but every soul in the Navy knows the truth, and one day justice will be served. Until then, Captain Price will be a wronged man, although it's not in his nature to be bitter about his fate."

I looked at Captain Price. He was politely listening to Miss Elliot, the perfect image of an attentive gentleman. He certainly didn't bear the expression of a resentful man who has been cheated of his well-deserved rewards.

Captain Price felt my stare, his eyes fell on mine and he smiled. I had met him before; I had no doubt about it.

The meal finished shortly afterwards, and the ladies retired to the drawing room. Once Lady Catherine, Lady Dalrymple, Miss Carteret and Miss Elliot had sat down for a game of pool, Mrs Wentworth approached me with a kind expression on her face.

"How are you finding London, Miss Darcy?"

"It is very different from Pemberley. The sheer amount of people is rather overwhelming."

She nodded, knowingly.

"I too miss the tranquillity of the countryside, but not for long. We are due to visit Admiral Croft and his wife, the Captain's sister, in Somersetshire. By a happy coincidence, they are settled in Kellynch, where I grew up. I am very much looking forward to seeing it again; it's a magnificent building surrounded by breathtaking scenery, although I suppose we all describe the places we love in similarly praising terms."

Mrs Wentworth gave me a gentle smile. I nodded. Her depiction of Kellynch sounded just like the one I might give of Pemberley. The big house was as close to my heart as any of my kin, my memory so intertwined with its existence that one might say it was part of me. I had spent endless hours of sheer happiness in the bright nursery, run along the corridors playing hide and seek, and counted the steps in the grand staircase over and over again in my childhood games. I had walked for miles in its gardens, soaked my feet in the stream, and fed the red fish in its many fountains. Alas, Pemberley was soon to become a paradise forever lost to me. My spirits turned melancholy, and Mrs Wentworth must have noticed because she changed the subject.

"However, my future is linked to the sea. I am planning to accompany the Captain in his foreign engagements, should they arise. Of course, many people, amongst them my father and sister, will despair at the fate of my poor skin, mercilessly exposed to the elements. That I may get freckles is the worst possible destiny in their eyes. But it is a price I'm prepared to pay for sharing my life with Captain Wentworth."

She said so with defiance and affection. Nobody could argue that she wasn't deeply in love with her husband.

Before I could reply, my aunt commanded my attention.

"Georgiana, will you play for us? It would give Lady Dalrymple, Miss Carteret and Miss Elliot great pleasure."

I excused myself and sat on the piano stool. The instrument was new and beautifully polished, the keys soft and shiny, as if they had been waxed. I started to play a bagatelle, a piece suitable for cards and conversation. The men entered shortly afterwards. Upon hearing me play, Don Cosimo came towards me and took a seat right next to the pianoforte. I blushed, trying to focus on the keys, but through the corner of my eyes, I could see him observing me, all rapt attention. After I had played the last key, Don Cosimo stood up and started to clap enthusiastically.

"*Brava!*" he shouted, and with great feeling added, "What musical ability you have, Miss Darcy. Music is one of the most marvellous joys in life, and seeing it performed by someone so talented is a true gift."

My cheeks were burning. I wanted to look away but couldn't; the green eyes weren't letting me go. Don Cosimo turned around to the rest of the guests. Captain Wentworth, his wife and Captain Price had clapped as well and were smiling in my direction. My aunt seemed pleased with the attention I was getting.

Miss Elliot and the lady of the house were busy with their game, but Miss Carteret had left the cards on the table and was looking towards me with clenched fists.

Don Cosimo theatrically swept the room with his arm.

"I am sure everyone in this drawing room is thinking the same. Look at that lovely lady; she is so musical, and so beautiful too!"

This time I looked away. I knew when someone took their compliments too far. But he wasn't waiving.

"May I suggest a duet next?"

I silently asked for my aunt's approval, and Lady Catherine, who had been observing us, discreetly nodded.

With a deft movement, Don Cosimo sat next to me, perused the music book on the music stand and decided on a page. Opening it wide, he put it in front of us.

"When you are ready, Miss Darcy," he said in a low voice.

I wasn't ready. Through my sheltered years at Pemberley, I had had very few opportunities to get so close to handsome strangers. Firmly planted on the same stool as me, I could feel the warmth of his body and smell his musky scent of clove and sandalwood. Wickham also used to smell of sandalwood. I felt my skin tingle. Would Don Cosimo notice the goosebumps? I hoped not.

We started to play. The melody he had picked was a gentle and joyful Irish dance, easy to hum and easier to play. Don Cosimo's fingers were deft on the keys, long but manly, with big, round nails topped with white crescents, just as they ought to be.

"You are a talented player, Miss Darcy," he muttered when he sensed I was comfortable with the rhythm. "I hope we will be able to enjoy many more duets together."

It was meant to be a trifle, a friendly comment, but it made me blush violently. A few moments later, Don Cosimo's voice again was a whisper in my ears, so close that his jaw was brushing my curls.

"Allow me to tell you that yours is the most beautiful complexion of all the ladies in the room."

It shames me to say so, but as clear-headed as I was in the face of Mr Collin's flattery, I was helpless when the same compliments were paid by a good-looking man with fine green eyes. Upon hearing his words, my face burned, and my insides trembled.

We finished the piece. This time, the claps were merely polite. Miss Carteret came towards us, her complexion a blotch of white and red.

"Miss Darcy, would you kindly take my place in the card game?" she said in a commanding voice. "You have been kind enough to play for us long enough and now deserve some rest. Don Cosimo, shall we perform another duet?"

Without waiting for his reply, she planted herself on the stool next to the prince, sitting closer to him than I had dared. Don Cosimo gave me a sheepish smile, then said something in Miss Carteret's ear that made her laugh coquettishly, her hand covering her mouth like a child's. Lady Dalrymple didn't even bother to glance in her daughter's direction. I saw that Captain Price had turned his back on the room and was looking out of one of the windows.

Miss Elliot smiled at me as I sat at the card table.

"Your duet with Don Cosimo was charming, Miss Darcy. I imagine you enjoyed it very much. But you must not take him too seriously. He has a reputation for being a tad eccentric. He has spent a lot of time in England, but he can't help being Italian, and their ways are rather different."

"Have you known Don Cosimo long, Miss Elliot?" I asked her.

"A while. I met him during my first season. He was still at Cambridge at the time. We became very fond of each other, and have remained good friends since."

My aunt seemed interested in the turn the conversation was taking.

"Miss Elliot, may I enquire, is there any particular reason why you didn't become more *intimately* acquainted with Don Cosimo at the time?"

Miss Elliot smiled, and fine lines appeared in her handsome face.

"You know what they say about Italian princes; they are a penny a dozen. And fancy leaving your family and country to live in such a backward place, with half of the comforts one may find in London or Bath!"

Lady Catherine seemed to be taken aback, but did not retreat.

"Nevertheless, Miss Elliot, I understand that Don Cosimo's family owns a palace so majestic that the Pope himself envies it," my aunt said with a deliberately indifferent tone of voice.

As her only response, Miss Elliot burst out laughing.

Chapter 10

The following day we were due to go to Almack's, the most elegant and exclusive assembly rooms in the country. Championed by ladies of the highest order in society, Almack's was reputedly the place where the most desirable matches were made, and Lady Catherine had pulled all the strings at her disposal to obtain two prized tickets to attend. For her, it was a most momentous occasion, and I knew better than to let her down.

I dressed in one of my new gowns, a dream of a garment made in soft silver satin with white lace over the sleeves and skirt. Jones had curled my hair tightly, and pretty ringlets framed my face, softening my features. On my collarbone, my mother's most exquisite diamond necklace shone brightly.

I entered my aunt's drawing room with my reticule clutched in my right hand, prepared for our departure. Lady Catherine was at her usual spot on the sofa, her lapdog sleeping on a cushion placed at her feet. The Colonel was facing her, his back to the door.

My aunt was the first one to see me.

"Ah, Georgiana, you are finally ready. Come closer."

I took a step in their direction, and Colonel Fitzwilliam turned to look at me. I saw his expression change in a split second, surprise appearing in his eyes as if he had seen me for the first time. Then, he slowly smiled and gave me a gentle nod.

Lady Catherine was also inspecting me, her gaze as severe as usual.

"Your maid has done a satisfactory job. You can tell she has been learning from Cosette."

Colonel Fitzwilliam, who hadn't yet uttered a word, was still observing me.

"Lady Catherine, may I escort you to Almack's?" he finally asked.

She cut him short.

"I am afraid it is impossible to gain entrance without an express invite of one of the patronesses, Colonel, and we do not have one for you. Moreover, you would put potential suitors off."

My cousin didn't reply.

"Of course, if what you wish for is a rich wife, I can assist you once Georgiana is engaged. I will find you the wealthiest and prettiest heiress in town so that you can join your cousin in the holy state of matrimony. You just have to wait, however.

Georgiana is in a hurry to get married. She must do so before she turns one-and-twenty, remember, whereas for you another few months are of little consequence."

Somewhat reluctantly, Colonel Fitzwilliam nodded, but he insisted on helping me board the barouche himself, and I sensed his gaze on me until the Grosvenor Square house disappeared from our view.

* * *

Although it was still rather early, the King Street establishment looked very busy, with at least two dozen carriages waiting at the entrance. Ladies and gentlemen, all most elegantly attired, were standing by the door clutching their tickets, and after a short wait, we too were ushered inside.

The interiors of Almack's were more pared back than I expected. The high-ceilinged rooms had large windows covered with plain velvet curtains, and large mirrors and simple pastoral paintings hung on the walls. I noticed with some disappointment that the crystal chandeliers were modest, definitely not large enough to make Mama's diamonds sparkle.

In the rooms it was warm, but not unpleasantly so. On the dance floor, a few couples were gracefully dancing the quadrille with the utmost elegance, their steps in perfect synchronicity. I watched them with admiration mixed with apprehension. My dancing skills had been much admired in Derbyshire, but whether they would prove becoming enough for the London *ton* remained to be seen.

My aunt quickly recognised an old acquaintance, a Lady Hamilton, the widow of a late cousin of hers, and they were soon engrossed in conversation. The music was cheery, and I was eager to dance. I looked around to see if I could recognise any familiar faces in the crowd, and to my surprise, I spotted Captain Price in a group of gentlemen. He saw me, smiled in my direction and, after some hesitation, approached us. He addressed my aunt, who was barely civil towards him. Then he spoke to me.

"May I have the honour of the next dance, Miss Darcy?"

I ignored Lady Catherine's frown and readily accepted. It would be an opportunity to find out once and for all why his countenance was so familiar to me. I also had to admit that I found his figure rather dashing. He wasn't perhaps as debonair as some of the other gentlemen of my acquaintance, but I felt an unyielding attraction towards his manly features, his big, strong hands, and his sincere blue eyes.

Captain Price was a fine dancer, agile and attuned to the music, and his movements were graceful. He was the first to speak.

"I am sorry we didn't get to converse more at Lady Dalrymple's. I was rather hoping you would be keen to continue to investigate our acquaintance some more."

I was surprised.

"So you admit that we have previously met! You must tell me how and when."

He gave me a half-smile.

"Have you forgotten all about your saviour? Young ladies are fickle indeed."

I looked at him with astonishment. The straight nose, the strong jaw, the piercing gaze.

He was the stranger at the inn!

The memory of the strength with which he had carried me to safety invaded me all of a sudden. His arms had been a haven after the commotion in the courtyard, his decisiveness a source of comfort, but he had lifted me without reserve, like a shepherd might carry a milkmaid, and I blushed at the recollection. At the same time, knowing the identity of my saviour came with more questions than answers. His attire on the day was not quite what one would expect from someone who frequented the most fashionable drawing rooms in London.

"If you're wondering at my appearance on that fateful day, I should explain that I was wearing my stable boy's coat," added Captain Price said with a teasing voice. "A fellow captain was due to attend a ceremony, his best coat was being mended, and I offered him the use of mine. However, I fear that the favour to an old friend lost me the respect of a new one."

"By no means!" I exclaimed.

He gave me a grave smile, then observed me in silence.

"I am glad to see that the wound has healed well."

I nodded.

"I followed your instructions. I still have your hip flask; I must return it to you."

"It certainly has been a faithful companion for many years. A lady very dear to me gave it to me to mark a particular occasion. I would be a happy man were I to have it back, but I also delight in the knowledge that it is safe in your fair hands."

My cheeks flushed. I paused, then plucked up the courage to ask the captain something that I had been wondering since polishing the hip flask.

"May I ask as for the lady and the reason of the commemoration?"

His brow creased, as if he the remembrance brought him pain.

"It was the day I was made first lieutenant under Captain Harvey at the *Leonidas*. It was going to be my great chance at progressing and making my fortune, and my very kind sister Fanny and her husband Mr Bertram presented me with an object to remember the date as a turning point for the better in my naval career. Unfortunately, things didn't quite go according to plan."

A shadow darkened his face for an instant. I thought of what Captain Wentworth had explained to me about the cowardly behaviour of Captain Harvey and the injustice it had brought upon his first lieutenant.

"I am sorry. I should not have asked."

"You have nothing to be sorry about. What was it that Burns said? The best laid schemes of mice and men..."

"... Gang aft agley, an' lea'e us nought but grief an'pain, for promis'd joy."

Captain Price looked at me with astonishment.

"Your Scotts is remarkable, Miss Darcy."

"My nursemaid came from Bonnyrigg."

"You are full of surprises, indeed."

The blue eyes were warm and friendly, and a wave of gratitude enveloped me.

"Captain Price, I owe you so much. It is a pity that my cousin isn't here; he would have been delighted to make your acquaintance and properly thank you for your assistance on that fateful day."

"Do you think so?"

Captain Price raised his eyebrow.

Perhaps not.

We continued to dance in silence, our steps in perfect synchronicity, my thoughts drifting. I had to admit that Captain Price's courageous heroics hadn't been properly acknowledged by Colonel Fitzwilliam. Whether it was because my cousin had been in shock at the time, or simply because he had taken my saviour to be a social inferior, I dared not guess.

That one's standing in society should mar the perception of their acts was an injustice. But life was unfair, was it not? I immediately remembered the three street urchins I had seen a few days before. The youngest one, I realised now, must have been Will's age. That one child should enjoy a comfortable life in the beautiful Pemberley surroundings, while the other was suffering the utmost destitution, was nothing short of tragic. My heart ached for the children on the street corner, and I resolved to find them the following morning.

Before I could speak again to my partner, the dance ended. Captain Price gave me a courteous bow and excused himself to rejoin his party, not before getting my assurances that I would dance with him again.

I turned to my aunt. I wanted to tell her about my previous encounter with Captain Price, but she silenced me with a look.

"Almack's is not what it used to be," she said with disgust, addressing Lady Hamilton. "How someone like Captain Price should be admitted, I do not know. I appreciate that some men in his profession become rich and are therefore granted access to certain circles, but I understand that his fortune is far from large."

"Lady Catherine, I do not credit my ears!" replied her friend with glee. "You do not know? Captain Price is a favourite nephew of Lady Bertram's and comes with glowing recommendations. Lady Bertram is rather a recluse and does not come to London often, preferring to spend most of her time at the family seat of Mansfield Park, but she is a *very* intimate friend of two of the current patronesses."

My aunt looked askance.

"He may have excellent sponsors, but that does not change the state of his financial affairs."

"Rumour has it that he has had to bear great injustices and that he may be wealthy one day if they are addressed," added Lady Hamilton lowering her voice.

I blushed. To hear Captain Price talked about in just terms of wealth and connections was prejudiced, even mean. I knew of his bravery, generosity and kindness towards those in need and I had been in receipt of them all. Surely his actions spoke more of his character than his relations and the money he had made in his profession?

Lady Hamilton had not finished.

"He is also a rather well-looking man," she said, winking in my direction. "Quite the hero, with the rugged appearance to match. And he has *very* good legs, if I may say so. They rather remind me of Lord Hamilton's at his age. Oh, but look, Lord Menzies! I must introduce you, Miss Darcy. Please come along..."

For the next two hours, I was paraded like a prize cow by my aunt and Lady Hamilton. I was introduced to and danced with two earls, a baronet, a fabulously wealthy plantation owner based in the West Indies who was looking for a wife to join him at the other end of the world, and the youngest son of a marquis. All, bar the plantation owner, had reasonably pleasant manners, but their agreeableness and dancing skills varied considerably, and they all paled in comparison with those of Captain Price.

Some time later, Captain Price came towards me again to claim the dance I had promised him, but this time my aunt intervened before I could accept.

"Captain Price, I am afraid my niece will have to decline your application. It is getting rather hot in here, and we need a refreshment."

The Captain offered to fetch us a drink or to accompany us to get some fresh air, but Lady Catherine stood up and shut him up with a gesture, dragging me with her.

I blushed at my aunt's discourtesy. Captain Price did not seem to take too much notice of her rude behaviour, but he did look disappointed. I excused myself, lowering my gaze. Perhaps later, I thought.

Lady Catherine and I headed to the supper rooms upstairs. The main hall had slowly filled up since our arrival and it was now rather noisy, but away from the musicians, the rooms were relatively quiet. A few patrons were scattered here and there, and on long tables covered by embroidered linens there were platters of dry cake and bread with butter to accompany the tea on offer.

My aunt made me sit in a corner hidden behind a column, away from the entrance.

"I cannot believe that, after seeing you in the company of so many men of consequence and wealth, that upstart sailor still feels entitled to ask to dance with you again!" Lady Catherine said in a whisper dripping with disdain. "You danced with him once because he is an acquaintance of some description, but you must make it very clear to him that he must not aspire to win a place in your affections. He is beneath your station."

I didn't see the Captain as my inferior, certainly not in matters of education or breeding. Perhaps his fortune was small, but he had much to commend him. As Captain Wentworth had said to me, Captain Price was an excellent man, and I no doubt about it.

The need to voice my opinion was stronger than my natural reserve.

"But Lady Hamilton said –"

"Lady Hamilton is extremely well connected, but she was always a terrible fantasist and cannot resist the lure of hopeless romance. As a result, she is also an abysmal matchmaker, one who delights in putting absurd ideas in young ladies' heads. Forget Captain Price. He will never do."

I drank my tea with resignation, but when my aunt suggested going downstairs again, I feigned a sudden headache and begged her to take me back to Grosvenor Square. The thought of having to humiliate Captain Price if he asked me again for a dance was too much. I had no right to offend him for causes unrelated to his good character. My aunt mumbled something about the ungratefulness of youth, but I pretended not to hear.

As we were leaving, I noticed for the first time a gentleman sitting on the other side of the large column. He had strawberry blond hair, a nose too small for his broad face and pale blue eyes. He was observing us with severity, and I wondered if he had overheard our conversation about Captain Price. I felt a wave of shame. Lowering my gaze, and praying that my suspicions were unfounded, I followed my aunt towards the exit.

Chapter 11

The following day, right after breakfast, I was in the parlour upstairs, immersed in a reverie of sweet memories from the previous afternoon, when my aunt's lapdog pushed the door open and came towards me, its tiny paws pitter-pattering on the waxed wooden floor. I took the little black fur ball in my arms and twirled with him around the room, whispering in its ears:

"Captain Price, and, although not as handsome as Don Cosimo, has much to commend him in terms of countenance and disposition, wouldn't you say?"

The dog gave me a sharp bark as if to remind me that my aunt believed he was not a suitable match. I stroked its silky fur.

"Don't be so grumpy! Did my brother not marry someone with a much smaller fortune than himself? I too should be able to do it, or at least daydream about it!"

But even as I was saying these words I knew that it was out of the question that I might follow the same path that Fitzwilliam had so resolutely taken. Oh, the unfairness of my sex!

Then there was a sudden knock on the door, and the pooch hid under my shawl. It was the footman, who entered with a letter for me on a silver tray. As soon as he left, I went towards the window to inspect the missive. It had been delivered by hand, but I didn't recognise the handwriting. I did, however, notice that the letter was scented with sandalwood.

I opened it with haste and read:

My dear Miss D.,

I have tried to ignore my feelings, but alas, I cannot. My heart still lightens at the memory of our playing together the other night. The joy it brought me I cannot describe, so attuned were our fingers, so together our hearts. Nothing would give me greater pleasure than seeing you again. I plan to visit my clock-maker at 17, South Molton Street tomorrow morning. I will be at the shop at 11 o'clock sharp. Your charming presence, even if just for an instant, would make me the happiest of men. I look forward to seeing your fair countenance again soon, and I know I will not be disappointed.

Forever your admirer,

C.

I had to sit down. My head was spinning. Don Cosimo had

put into words what I had sensed during our duet; that he should feel the same was rather extraordinary. As if noticing my confused state, the little dog gave a hollow bark and started licking my hands. I sat it on my lap, absentmindedly stroking its back, and read the letter again.

This second time, I noticed a hint of discomfort rising from the pit of my stomach. Don Cosimo's plans demanded secrecy, but I had been dragged into deception in the past and did not intend to follow suit again.

I gently put the lapdog on the floor, stood up and went towards the fireplace with Don Cosimo's letter clutched in my hand. The weather was warmer, but my aunt insisted that no expense should be spared in ensuring the comfort of her Grosvenor Square lodgings, and as a result, the servants kept the fires going in the two drawing rooms as well as the parlour. I watched the flames dance for a few moments, feeling the warmth from the hearth against my skin.

I knew what I had to do. I could not afford the slightest shadow on my reputation, especially not after my close encounter with danger those years ago. I slowly brought over the scented letter to the flames. My skin was burning now, so close were my fingers to the fire, but with a sigh, I dropped my hand at the last minute. I couldn't bring myself to destroy it. After erasing all trace of Wickham's correspondence, Don Cosimo's note was the only letter of admiration I had left, the only tangible proof that I, too, could command affection. I looked at it with despair. It was like a hot coal against my palm, and too dangerous to have it with me.

I ran upstairs and hid it at the bottom of the trunk, right next to Captain Price's hip flask, covering it with enough petticoats to dress a small army of ladies.

* * *

I had arranged to collect Mrs Gardiner and the Misses Bennet from Gracechurch Street the ensuing morning. The day was bright, with only the faintest whisper of clouds in the sky, and the sun felt warm against my skin. Kitty was looking out the window when I got to the Gardiners' residence in Cheapside, and she waved in my direction as soon as she saw me, an excited look on her face. I waved back. Moments later, Kitty boarded the barouche with delight, followed by her aunt and sister.

"It is such a *pretty* carriage, Miss Darcy! You don't know how blessed you are to own it!"

"Miss Darcy, I feel obliged to clarify that our uncle's carriage is perfectly adequate, although this one does have a very pleasing shape," added Mary in a rather grandiose tone. "You are fortunate indeed."

I smiled inwardly. In her eagerness to appear educated, Mary rather reminded me of her cousin, Mr Collins.

"I thank you, but I must admit that I am not its lucky owner. The barouche is Lady Catherine's."

At the mention of my aunt's name, Kitty opened her eyes

wide, and her posture stiffened. Mary, who had her hand on the inside handle of the door, moved it immediately to her lap. I suspected that the Misses Bennet found the prospect of sitting in Lady Catherine's drawing-room for an hour less than appealing. No wonder that my suggestion to ride into town with them had been so warmly received.

Mrs Gardiner broke the ensuing silence to discuss Elizabeth's health. She had received a letter from Mrs Bingley the day before assuring her that my sister-in-law was feeling better.

"Mrs Darcy was always a strong and energetic child, and I am sure she will recover. However, I feel for her. Miss Darcy, you know her and her love of the outdoors. A forced early confinement must be the worst of tortures for her."

"Life is full of suffering, Aunt," intervened Mary with a solemn face. "One might say that Lizzy has been spared her share until now, and is just beginning to pay her dues."

"Mary, really, there is no need to use that language, it is not very becoming in a young lady," Mrs Gardiner gently reproached her before turning to me. "So, where do you wish us to accompany you today, Miss Darcy?"

"My maidservant insists that I need new slippers."

"Well, I know a little shop just a couple of streets from here…"

Mary and Kitty looked at their aunt with disappointment.

"Although, of course, there are many more options in town," added Mrs Gardiner. "Perhaps you have one in mind already."

I bit my bottom lip. I thought of Don Cosimo's green eyes and my insides trembled. Surely there could be no harm in observing him from a distance? He didn't have to see me.

"I have been told that there is a good establishment in South Molton Street."

"Indeed, I know just the one. It has a beautiful assortment of all sorts of wares. Mary, Kitty, you do not require anything just now, do you?"

The Misses Bennet immediately started to speak at the same time, explaining their need for new ribbons and disagreeing as to whose gowns and bonnets required the most attention. Mary deftly justified her want for adornment as selfless consideration towards others in wanting to appear neatly dressed, but Kitty's impassioned defence of the appalling state of her wardrobe was winning. I made the most of the confusion to look out of the carriage window and enjoy a view of the buzzing streets.

As we turned yet another corner, I suddenly remembered the orphans. I had forgotten about them in spite of my resolve; I should be ashamed. I put my hand in my reticule. I had some coins with me. I would order the driver to stop as soon as I saw the unfortunate children; Mrs Gardiner's pious heart would not object to me giving them some alms. I stretched my neck to look for the urchins amongst the crowds, but the path we followed was new, and I did not recognise any landmarks until we were within walking distance of our destination. I told myself that perhaps we would see them on the way back, and the prospect comforted me.

South Molton Street was very busy. The coachman left us at the Oxford Street corner, and I asked him to pick us up an hour later. The clock of a church spire rising above the roofs informed me that it was almost half past ten. Walking gingerly, the only way it was possible in the company of excitable Kitty, we went into the shop Mrs Gardiner had mentioned.

I perused the varied array of slippers on display and quickly chose four pairs in assorted colours. Jones would be pleased. As the Misses Bennet were deciding which items to buy, I looked outside. Across from the shop there were a number of establishments designed to appeal to the well-heeled. One in particular immediately caught my eye. It was a clock-maker, with a big golden sign over the door announcing the trade and a large cuckoo clock on the shop window.

I narrowed my eyes. There was a number 17 painted in gold leaf above the door. My heart began to pound louder and louder. I took a deep breath.

Will he come? And if he does, will I be brave enough to make my presence known?

I thought of the possible consequences of the encounter. Even if word got out that I had met Don Cosimo, no one would question that I should run into him on South Molton Street. He was, after all, a man of taste and consequence, and the shops in the area catered to the aristocracy as well as the gentry. Nevertheless, my hands were slightly trembling when Kitty joined me.

"What are you observing with so much interest, Miss Darcy?

Oh, I see! What a delightful cuckoo clock! I love cuckoo clocks. What time is it?"

I checked the church spire and felt a jolt inside.

"It's five minutes until 11 o'clock."

"Aunt, Mary, hurry up! There's a cuckoo clock across the road we must go and see! It will go off in five minutes!"

Mary, who still hadn't selected her ribbons, grumbled but followed suit, and we all stepped out of the shop and headed towards the clock-maker, just a few yards away, ostensibly in order to humour Kitty.

My heart was now as loud as a canon, and I wondered why nobody else seemed to hear it.

The shop had the widest glass panel I had ever seen. On the other side, a thousand beautiful objects veered for the attention of the passers-by, but without a doubt, the cuckoo clock was the display centrepiece. It was a work of wonder, an exquisite alpine-style house with little tables and miniature patrons enjoying a happy drink in the sun. Just outside the delightful wooden building, a brass band was playing, their tiny instruments perfect replicas of their normal-sized counterparts.

Discreetly, I observed the dark shades inside the shop, just visible from outside, but I couldn't distinguish much more than vague silhouettes.

We heard the church bells first and then the clock started to chime. With the last ding, the tiny band began to play a merry tune, the doors and windows of the little building opened, and out came four pairs of tiny wooden dancers, spinning around the house and its balcony.

Kitty and Mary let out cries of delight at the spectacle, but I wasn't looking at the clock anymore. My sight was fixed on a pair of eyes behind the glass. Almond-shaped eyes with dark eyelashes, just like Wickham's.

I felt a surge of joy mixed with fear in my veins.

Don Cosimo smiled and immediately came out of the shop.

"Miss Darcy, what a *surprise* to see you!" he cried with the grandest of gestures. "I trust you are in good health?"

I replied that I was, and answered his civil questions as to the wellbeing of my aunt. Then, he lowered his voice so that only I could hear it.

"You make me the happiest of men by coming to find me today," he whispered. "Allow me to believe that you derive as much pleasure from seeing me as I do from beholding you."

My chest trembled.

Mrs Gardiner and the Misses Bennet had lost all interest in the cuckoo clock and were looking at me and the prince expectantly. A conversation longer than a few minutes would raise their suspicions.

"I am afraid I must go," I muttered.

"When will I see you again? I beg you, give me an answer."

"Are you invited to Lady Dalrymple's ball next Friday?"

"I am, indeed. But it is still many days away. Your aunt is hosting a dinner on Monday, is she not?"

He smiled, giving me a knowing look. Then, he bowed most gallantly, turned around to nod in the direction of my companions, and went back into the shop.

Kitty was the first one to talk.

"Who was he, Miss Darcy?"

"Don Cosimo Giovanni Ludovico, Prince of Rasiglia and Ponziano," I answered in a daze.

"A prince! I knew it. He looks just like royalty ought to look!" she cried.

"Italian princes are not technically royalty," added Mary.

"Oh, Miss Darcy, he is dreamy! He must be rich as well, going into that shop."

"Mary, Kitty, I believe Lady Catherine's coachman has been waiting for us long enough. We do not want to upset him – or his mistress. Let's go."

Mrs Gardiner clearly didn't allow herself to be impressed by a title or a foreign national, no matter how green his eyes and elegant his appearance. With that said, we headed back to the meeting point previously agreed with the coachman.

On the way back to Grosvenor Square I deliberately ignored the enquiring looks of the Bennet ladies and opted instead to look out of the window. I was in turmoil. It was uncanny how similar Don Cosimo's countenance was to that of the man I had loved. But was my new acquaintance the real object of my attraction or did I just long for the attention of someone capable of stepping into the memory of Wickham? I couldn't answer that question. I prayed that time would give me perspective and clarity.

On the way back I asked the coachman to drive past the corner where we had seen the street children a few days before, but there was no sight of them. An old man with a long filthy beard and a wooden leg had taken their spot. I felt foolish. It was silly to expect that they should still be there, waiting for my coins. Disappointed, I sighed, the coins in my reticule burning like the brightest fire.

Chapter 12

Lady Catherine seemed as satisfied as a well-fed cat upon hearing that I had run into Don Cosimo on South Molton Street. Colonel Fitzwilliam, on the contrary, appeared somewhat alarmed, his eyebrows arched, his fists clenched, but didn't say a word about the encounter.

As for me, I was torn in two. To myself, I had to admit a natural inclination for Captain Price, but as Lady Catherine had already pointed out, my feelings must not be allowed to develop into real affection, because his cause as potential suitor was a lost one. At the same time, Don Cosimo stirred intense and tangled emotions inside of me. Under his gaze, I felt beautiful and lovable, but the memory of our last encounter was tainted with guilt. Had I not met him behind my family's back? However much I tried to convince myself that I had done nothing wrong, that Don Cosimo had behaved most honourably towards me, and that ours was just the kind of gallant flirtation that worldly ladies have all the time, the secrecy troubled me.

That same evening, the footman brought another note in the handwriting I immediately recognised as Don Cosimo's. I brought the letter to my nose. It was scented, just like last time. I ripped it open as soon as the servant had left the room and read:

My dearest Miss D.,

I thank you, my fair lady, for answering the call of this poor man desperate to behold you. We must meet again. I will go for a ride in Hyde Park tomorrow afternoon. You must find a suitable excuse and partner to join me there. Once we set eyes on each other, I will find a way to speak to you. I look forward to seeing your fair countenance again soon.

Your faithful servant,

C.

I sensed a wave of happiness mixed with distress. Don Cosimo wanted to see me again. His request for concealment clashed once more with what I believed was right, but the pull his eyes had over me was too hard to ignore. I considered my options. Lady Catherine did not enjoy going out in the afternoon, much preferring the morning for outings in her barouche. She certainly wouldn't agree to a ride in the park.

There was only one other course of action.

I folded the letter carefully and stashed it at the bottom of the trunk, with Don Cosimo's other note and Captain Prince's hip flask. As dangerous as it was to keep the letters amongst my belongings, they were at least easy to destroy. The flask, however, was equally compromising, and a whole other matter. If my cousin or my aunt found it amongst my undergarments, I would have to give many unpleasant explanations. I had to do something about it, and soon. With determination, I shut the trunk and dressed for dinner.

* * *

It was to be a quiet evening, with just the three of us dining in the house. When I went downstairs with Lady Catherine, my cousin was already waiting. He had been away and I had not seen him for a few days, but he appeared to be delighted to be back. He came towards us with open arms.

"My dear ladies! It is a pleasure to be able to join you for dinner tonight. It has been a busy few weeks for me, and I apologise for not having spent as much time in your company as I would have desired."

I smiled and nodded, but my aunt wasn't so easily mollified.

"We are glad to have you with us, Colonel. However, your lack of attentiveness of late has been most disconcerting. I ignore the nature of the affairs that have been keeping you away from us, although I have my suspicions. However, I fully expect you not to neglect us as much in future. As the only man in the house, it is your duty to escort us."

"Of course, Lady Catherine," he said, looking mildly uncomfortable. Then, turning towards me, he asked, "Georgiana, have you seen many of the sights the capital city has to offer?"

It was my chance. I gave Colonel Fitzwilliam an account of my outings since arriving in London, detailing the places and attractions I had been to, gently leading him to the point that interested me.

"Believe it or not, Cousin, I have yet to visit Hyde Park, although it is just around the corner. I have been told that it is a most excellent place for getting fresh air and exercise."

Colonel Fitzwilliam bit the bait.

"Lady Catherine, have you not taken Georgiana to Hyde Park yet?"

My aunt glanced towards me with indifference.

"She can walk there with her maidservant anytime."

I could feel my hopes disappear, but my cousin intervened with his usual charm.

"But where is the enjoyment in that, Lady Catherine? I am sure Georgiana is thinking of going for a ride in the afternoon, when the most refined society take to the park in their best attires, horses and carriages. It is quite a spectacle, one that everyone should behold at least once in a lifetime, would you not agree?"

I plucked up the courage to intervene.

"If I could borrow your barouche again, aunt, I could invite

Mrs Gardiner and the Misses Bennet to join me. I know they would be delighted."

My aunt shrugged her shoulders.

"I find all that parading rather *vulgar*, but I suppose it will do you good to be seen. Just make sure you wear your wide parasol, and do not expect me to join you."

I could have embraced her.

"Of course Aunt."

"That's all settled then," she said, dismissing me with a wave of her hand. "I will ask Waller to wax the barouche especially for the occasion."

Colonel Fitzwilliam observed me with tenderness.

"I can tell you are delighted with the prospect of the Hyde Park excursion, Georgiana." He was gently squeezing my hand. "You know how to appreciate the simple things in life, and that is one of the reasons why I admire you so."

I smiled faintly in his direction, then addressed Lady Catherine again.

"I thank you, Aunt. I will write to Mrs Gardiner at once."

My cousin's brow creased.

"Mrs Gardiner? No, there will be but two spaces left in the barouche. Let's invite Mr and Mrs Collins instead."

I looked at the Colonel, my mouth agape. That he might want to accompany me to Hyde Park had not even crossed my mind. After all, he had avoided most social engagements with my aunt or myself since arriving in town.

He took my hand to his mouth and kissed it. I coloured deeply, confused by his gesture.

"But you needn't worry about it, dear Georgiana. I will take care of it."

With a heavy heart, I bit the inside of my cheeks so as not to let my disappointment show.

* * *

Although not in the manner I had anticipated, the following afternoon I was riding in Hyde Park in my aunt's barouche. London had the grey tinge of cloudy days and it appeared to be in need of a good scrub, as if the maid in charge of keeping it clean was losing her eyesight and couldn't quite see the dust build-up. In spite of the weather, there were many carriages, their passengers out to see and be seen. It was quite a sight. Ladies and gentlemen were wearing their most elegant afternoon clothes, in a parade of the latest fashions from Paris and the Continent. Chaises, phaetons, landauettes and curricles crowded the broad avenues of the park, some with brightly coloured livery, all impeccably shiny even under the miserable sky.

Mr Collins was in good spirits. He only ceased to praise Lady Catherine's generosity when we arrived at the gates of the park and he entered a tirade on the vainness and shallowness of some human hearts. Immediately afterwards, he pointed to a particularly ornate-looking curricle.

"Mrs Collins, I wonder if we should look into acquiring one of such vehicles once we move to our future home. I will require a rapid means of transport to get to my parishioners, and the Longbourn income should allow amply for this kind of expense, do you not think?"

Mrs Collins started to explain, in the most diplomatic way possible, that it would be best to wait before making any plans, probably much aware that achieving what her husband was so openly discussing required the death of my beloved sister-in-law's father. But I was barely listening to what they were saying. Instead, I was looking around with eagerness, to see if I could locate Don Cosimo nearby.

The crowd was much larger than I had anticipated. There were scores of gentlemen and even some ladies on horseback, but I didn't recognise the prince among them. Perhaps Don Cosimo preferred to go in his carriage, but there were so many. Then I realised: I did not know what his livery colours were. Lady Catherine, Mrs Gardiner, even Mrs Wickham would have known to ask the footman before leaving the house, but the thought had not even occurred to me.

After some minutes of observation, I, at last, identified one of the riders, on a magnificent white stallion. It wasn't Don Cosimo but Captain Wentworth. He recognised me, nodded in my direction and approached our barouche with a broad smile, which I immediately returned. My cousin was looking at him with some suspicion.

"Captain Wentworth, allow me to introduce my cousin, Colonel Fitzwilliam, and Mr and Mrs Collins," I quickly said.

Cousin Fitzwilliam seemed to immediately relax and eagerly extended his hand.

"Captain Wentworth, it is a pleasure to finally meet you. I have heard many good things about you and your lovely wife."

Two other gentlemen on horseback approached us. Captain Price came first, his broad-shouldered silhouette enhanced by his powerful mount. He was looking more attractive than I remembered, his blue eyes piercing in the daylight, and my whole body tingled upon seeing him. Unfortunately, my spirits took a turn for the worse upon recognising the second rider, who turned out to be the red-haired fellow that I suspected had witnessed my conversation with Lady Catherine at Almack's. I was mortified. I lowered my gaze, praying that my fears were unfounded.

Unaware of my embarrassment, Captain Wentworth introduced Captain Price and the second gentleman, a Captain Lowry. Captain Lowry gave me a serious look, but Captain Price seemed his usual frank self. I felt a wave of relief. It didn't look like his friend had informed him of what he had witnessed two days prior.

After some initial conversation, my cousin addressed Captain Price.

"Have we met before, Captain? I believe I recognise you."

"I assure you that we haven't been introduced, Colonel," Captain Price tersely answered, "but it's a pleasure to make your acquaintance."

I smiled at his words, and he noticed, for he smiled as well.

Colonel Fitzwilliam quickly learnt that Captain Wentworth was as keen a sportsman as himself, and what followed was a lively conversation between the two about the best conditions for the hunt, the kind of weapons preferred, the largest pieces captured and the skills and obedience of their respective pointers.

While this was going on, I discreetly observed Captain Price. He took it as an invite to speak to him, and approached me with a smile.

"Miss Darcy, I believe I met some close family connections of yours the other day at a military ball. I see the look of surprise on your face, but I assure you, soldiers and sailors do mix on occasion. The three ladies in question were Mrs Wickham, who I understand is married to an officer, Miss Bennet and Miss Catherine Bennet."

So Lydia had not remained at Pemberley long. That her sisterly affection for Elizabeth should not extend to looking after her when she was unwell should not have come as a surprise. Nevertheless, at the mention of her, my heart stopped. I could not help but wonder if her husband was with her, but I forced myself to appear perfectly composed and not say a word on the matter.

"We didn't speak long," continued the Captain, "but Mrs Wickham promptly informed me that Pemberley was the home of her sister, Mrs Darcy. I immediately thought of you and mentioned that we were acquainted."

A shiver of pleasure tingled down my spine.

So he had thought of me.

"Mrs Wickham also told me that her husband spent his childhood in Pemberley, due to him being the son of your father's steward. That she should be doubly connected to your family's ancestral home is an extraordinary coincidence, is it not?"

I reddened. It was unpleasant to be reminded that Lydia enjoyed boasting about her Pemberley connections at every opportunity, but I managed to remain calm.

"She is a very charming lady," added Captain Price, unaware of my distress.

His words twisted my insides, and for an instant I wished that Mr Collins had overheard Captain Price's comments and was compelled to intervene. However, my aunt's vicar was busy observing the wealth and rank of passers-by and providing his wife with a running commentary on who was who.

Captain Price tried to engage me further in conversation, but all my appetite for his company had vanished. He seemed confused. I noticed Captain Lowry look at him with concern, then turn towards me with his brow creased.

Meanwhile, my cousin seemed very pleased with Captain Wentworth.

"It is tremendously enjoyable to find men who are so fond of hunting, Captain. I find that some of the company one encounters in London is more interested in less wholesome pursuits. My aunt, Lady Catherine de Bourgh, is hosting a dinner party on Tuesday night and I am sure she would be delighted if the three of you and Mrs Wentworth were kind enough to join us. I must show you the splendid hunting gun I bought recently. It is superb for bird shooting."

I looked at my cousin with some alarm, but it was too late: Captain Wentworth readily accepted the invitation and Captain Price also assented, searching for my gaze immediately afterwards. I couldn't return it. I was looking at Captain Lowry, who gave his friend a sideway glance, before also agreeing to the plan.

We said goodbye to the captains and the barouche took us for another leap around the park. I didn't see Don Cosimo, nor was I able to look for him, for I was busy answering my cousin's questions about the gentlemen we had just met. He was particularly impressed by Captain Wentworth.

"A pleasant sort of fellow. There are many like him in the Navy. They have a tough job, but he appears to have done very well for himself. Not all sailors get to marry a baronet's daughter. How much do you say he has?"

I blushed. I found discussing one or one's friends' wealth a weary topic of conversation, no matter how generally acceptable it was. Nevertheless, I gave the Colonel the information he required, and he seemed pleased with my answers. He then moved on to Captain Price and began to say how convinced he was that their paths had crossed previously. Just like me, he was incapable of associating the distinguished Navy captain we had just met, his dress carefully starched, his horse beautifully brushed, with the ragged man who had come to my assistance at the inn. I could have spoken then, but I kept quiet. My delicacy prevented me from bringing up a circumstance that would embarrass my cousin greatly, so Captain Price's identity continued to be a shared secret between my saviour and me.

We left Mr and Mrs Collins back in their rooms and arrived at Grosvenor Street hungry, but delighted with the outing. Lady Catherine, just as I had imagined, was none too happy upon hearing that Colonel Fitzwilliam had extended an invitation on her behalf to Captain Wentworth and his friends.

"Oh, I do not object to Captain Wentworth. He is a very elegant man, and his wife is Lord Elliot's daughter. Hers is a very respectable family. However, that Captain Lowry is a perfect stranger, even if you say that his manners are pleasant. And I do not like seeing Captain Price near Georgiana."

"How so, Lady Catherine? He is a nice enough fellow, and of course he will be perfectly aware that she is well out of his station."

"Young men get funny ideas these days, Colonel. The rules are not as clearly drawn as they were in my day. But you are right. If he is as bright as he seems, he will know that Georgiana will not even consider him. Now, we will need more ladies to even out the numbers, but at such short notice I am not sure we will be able to find any."

Colonel Fitzwilliam suggested inviting Mr and Mrs Gardiner and the Misses Bennet. After a long silence, Lady Catherine sighed.

"I suppose they will have to do."

Later, when I was in the parlour, a servant discreetly handed me a scented note in the now familiar handwriting.

My most darling Miss D.,

This afternoon I had the immense pleasure of beholding your delightful face in Hyde Park. The joy in my heart I cannot describe for want of words. That you have again responded to my plea makes me the happiest of men.

My felicity was only marred by the fact that you did not appear to see me. I dared not approach your carriage when I saw you were in the company of your cousin, but I imagine his presence was probably as unwelcome to you as it was to me.

I ache to lose myself in your eyes again. I long to see you tomorrow at your aunt's, and dance with you, and see you once more, cara mia.

Your eternal servant,

C.

I felt my cheeks burn and a butterfly tighten in my belly. Things were getting out of hand. This time I made a bundle of Don Cosimo's note and threw it in the fire.

Chapter 13

The day of Lady Catherine's dinner, the Grosvenor Square household was a flurry of activity. Servants rushed around carrying silverware, flowers and cleaning cloths, the maids and menservants working together like a well-drilled army under the direction of Dewars, the butler. I kept myself to my room, and allowed Cosette and Jones to get on with their work. My aunt had been most particular in her instructions: I was to look radiant. For my aunt, tonight was the night.

Lady Catherine had invited a large party of friends and acquaintances. As well as the social circle we had frequented of late, she also asked two of the gentlemen who had danced with me at Almack's. The first one was Sir Leach, a newly-widowed baronet who had a melancholy air about him and who, in spite of his relative youth, had barely a wisp of hair left on his head. The second gentleman was Lord Ebrington, whose father was Marquis

Ebrington. According to my aunt, he was one of the most eligible bachelors in town, and although I did not doubt his suitability on paper, I did not find his thick girth and unpleasant laugh particularly appealing.

Of course, Don Cosimo would also attend. Following my outing with Mrs Gardiner and the Misses Bennet, I had timidly suggested inviting him, and my aunt thought it a marvellous idea. Lady Catherine seemed genuinely delighted to have three potential suitors for my hand under her roof. With no restraint, she spoke to my cousin over breakfast of her plans.

"You see, by throwing them all together, they will have no other option than to demonstrate the extent of their interest. Nothing like a cock fight to weed out the serious contenders from the time wasters. By the end of the night, we will have a favourite, mark my words."

My cousin looked slightly alarmed.

"But dear Lady Catherine, what do we know of the gentlemen?"

"All that is necessary, Colonel. Sir Leach is titled, rich and in need of a wife to give him a male heir and his two young daughters a mother figure. Lord Ebrington is the first son of a Marquis, in line to inherit his father's title, and, therefore, an excellent prospect. Admittedly, he is not the most pleasant of gentlemen, but knowing what is customary in the upper echelons of society, Georgiana would not see him that often once married. He might even leave her in peace altogether once she gives him an heir and a spare."

"Lady Catherine, are those comments necessary?"

"Don't be a prude, Colonel. Georgiana has been sheltered from the ways of the world in Pemberley, but if she is to marry well, the sooner she understands how things work, the better."

My aunt then turned to me with a grimace.

"And of course, there will also be Don Cosimo, whom I dare say is already a favourite of Georgiana's. An Italian prince with an ancient title, who belongs to a most distinguished aristocratic lineage. The family estate is said to be beautiful, but I bet you it is crumbling. He will need to marry into money, and Georgiana fits the bill perfectly."

I blushed. My aunt gave a gesture of displeasure with her hand.

"Lady Hamilton insists that Don Cosimo will never marry a commoner and that he is already spoken for, but I noticed the way he was looking at you the other day, Georgiana."

If only she knew about the letters in the trunk, I thought. I lowered my gaze, hoping that she would not probe me any further.

The day flew by, and before I knew it, I was downstairs, wearing a pale pink satin gown that, according to Jones, perfectly enhanced my complexion. Mr and Mrs Collins were the first guests to enter the main door at Grosvenor Square. Mr Collins was as deferential as ever, but my aunt barely paid him any notice, so immersed was she in bossing her servants around with her final instructions. Mr and Mrs Gardiner and the Misses Bennet arrived next, Kitty visibly excited, Mary looking as if she had been dragged out of Cheapside against her will. Lady Dalrymple and Miss Carteret, the Elliots and the Wentworths entered all at the same time, and they were soon followed by Captain Price and Captain Lowry.

Captain Price's behaviour was entirely proper on arrival, but I quickly realised that he was avoiding my gaze. Captain Lowry, acting as his shadow, held his head high and looked at me with cold eyes. Judging by his behaviour, I feared that he had finally shared my aunt's opinions with his friend. A wave of shame invaded me, but I had little time to reflect on it, for my duty was to stand with my aunt and my cousin by the door, welcoming our guests.

When I had the chance to look around the drawing room, I noticed that Captain Price and Captain Lowry were talking to the Misses Bennet on very amicable terms. I reminded myself that they were casual acquaintances, but I couldn't help noticing that Captain Price and Kitty seemed to be particularly intimate. Perhaps it was the matching grave air of Captain Lowry and Mary Bennet right next to them, but they appeared to be perfectly matched conversationalists.

Lady Hamilton finally arrived, her complexion flushed from climbing the stairs, her gaze darting around to take everything in. Right behind her came Don Cosimo. He was wearing a green coat that matched his eyes, and he looked every inch the fairy tale prince. He saw me straightaway, a complicit smile on his lips. In spite of myself, I felt enveloped by butterflies, my skin tickled by a thousand feathers. He courteously bowed to my cousin and the older women, then took my hand and brought it to his lips. The intimate gesture was completely unexpected, and I coloured deeply.

I reflected on Don Cosimo's letters and my deliberate attempts to encounter him by following his instructions. It was natural that he should feel entitled to kiss my hand. When he had excused himself to mingle with the rest of the guests, my aunt gave Lady Hamilton a knowing look, but her friend's gaze was fixed on the prince's back.

"Such a *handsome* man!" she said, in a trembling voice. "A fabulous catch, too, even if the family fortunes have been in decline for some time. However, Lady Catherine, do *not* get any ideas. He comes from an ancient and proud family and he shall *never* be convinced to enter matrimony with a commoner. Do not say that I did not warn you, my dear friend!"

"We will see."

My aunt's words were sharp as daggers.

Colonel Fitzwilliam had not said a word, but he was looking very pale suddenly.

* * *

After dinner, Kitty insisted that there should be some dancing. Her eagerness was such that my aunt could but give her assent, and the arrangements were promptly made to accommodate half a dozen couples in the second drawing room. Mrs Wentworth volunteered to play, and soon after the house was enveloped in music.

My first dance was with Sir Leach, who remained silent most of the time. He was a good enough dancer, so at least I had that consolation. Lord Ebrington danced with me next, but just like at Almack's, his steps were a few seconds too late and his movements too harsh to be considered elegant. Meanwhile, Captain Price danced with Kitty, who seemed to be having the time of her life. He had not spoken to me all night, and it was as if in spite of the intimacy of some of our prior conversations, we were strangers again.

Don Cosimo was nowhere to be seen. I had last spotted him talking to Miss Carteret, shortly after the gentlemen had joined us ladies in the drawing room; I had been busy humouring my aunt and speaking to the men she intended me to fall in love with, and I had not noticed him come and go. Then, out of the blue, he appeared and asked me if I would join him for the next dance. Miss Carteret was right behind him, her chignon loose and her gaze content, and his green coat looked slightly dishevelled, but I didn't even wonder why. Feeling Lady Catherine's gaze on my shoulders, I assented.

Before Mrs Wentworth could start playing another tune, Don Cosimo approached her and murmured something in her ear. She blushed and looked at her husband, who promptly joined them.

Once told what the matter was, Captain Wentworth came towards my aunt, his handsome face grave.

"Lady Catherine, Don Cosimo has asked for a particular tune for the next dance."

"Does your wife not know how to play it?" asked Lady Catherine with little patience.

"I am afraid she would rather not," the Captain answered tersely. "The Prince has requested a waltz."

"A waltz!" exclaimed Lady Hamilton with a smirk on her face. My aunt stifled a gasp, although she quickly recovered her composure.

I had heard of waltzing, of course. I had even played some pieces, and my fingers had enjoyed the soft cadence of their dancing on the keys of the Pemberley pianoforte. I also knew that it had been received with some scandal, and that it had not been acceptable to dance it in polite society for some time. The reason of the ban I could not fathom; I had never seen a waltz danced before. However, Don Cosimo was determined about his choice of dance. He addressed my aunt with confidence.

"Lady Catherine, there is no reason for such alarm. In recent times the waltz has been readily embraced by the higher echelons of society and is now widely danced in the most elegant London circles, although admittedly mostly in private. Captain Wentworth need not act with such reserve."

Captain Wentworth, with profound dignity, defended himself.

"I am afraid that you will have to excuse my wife. She will not be performing it."

Don Cosimo dismissed the Captain's concerns.

"Your wife's delicacy is surprisingly prudish for a baronet's daughter. No problem, we will find another player."

Captain Wentworth's knuckles whitened, and Mrs Wentworth put her hand on his arm. The atmosphere was tense. My aunt was following the exchange with an alarmed expression, but Lady Hamilton seemed to enjoy herself. Not bothered in the slightest by the situation, Don Cosimo looked around the room. Then, with a smile, he addressed Mary.

"Ah, Miss Bennet! I understand you play the pianoforte?"

Mary, delighted to be the centre of attention, promptly volunteered to replace Mrs Wentworth at the instrument, her hands ready to play.

Don Cosimo offered his arm to me. Until that point, I had not realised that he still intended me to join him on the dance floor.

"Don Cosimo, I'm afraid I cannot be able to be your partner," I stuttered, "I have never danced the waltz."

"My dear Miss Darcy, I assure you that there are no secrets to the waltz if you allow an experienced partner to lead you. I am a rather gifted dancer, as you will see."

Confused, I searched for Lady Catherine gaze. My aunt reluctantly nodded.

The prince took my hand, led me to the dance floor and positioned me there, my arms wide open as if I was a statue of

Venus in a Roman garden. We were the only couple willing to dance, so all eyes set on us, and I felt rather foolish. Don Cosimo looked at me, his gaze the purest of greens, and gave me an irresistible smile.

Mary Bennet's cumbersome fingers began to play. Then, Don Cosimo put his right hand on my waist and took my other hand with the utmost delicacy, as if it was a precious treasure. I almost shrieked from the surprise of his embrace.

"Just let yourself go," he whispered into my ear.

And I did.

The butterflies, the feathers, they all came back with a vengeance. I could feel Don Cosimo's body through the thin satin of my dress. He was spinning me around as if I was a water lily being taken for a ride by the capriciousness of the water currents. In spite of my initial shock at having a man stand so close to me, what followed was the pure joy of dancing. In no small measure due to Don Cosimo's talent at guiding my steps, we quickly became attuned to each other, like a four-armed dancer joined at the hip. The music was fast, our movements nimble and elegant. I was in heaven.

Then, it was over. The reverberations of the last key were like the start of a funeral. I looked up. Don Cosimo was smiling at me, soft black waves framing his chiselled features.

"I wonder if you know what they say about those who dance well together," he whispered into my ear.

I didn't, but his voice implied all sorts of things. I blushed, unable to answer.

Don Cosimo returned me to my aunt, who was pale, her shock plain in her grey eyes. Colonel Fitzwilliam, who had briefly left the room, was looking in my direction with alarm. Lady Hamilton, on the contrary, seemed delighted with the spectacle. Across the room, I caught Captain Price's eye. He was still with Kitty, but he wasn't smiling anymore. His brow was creased, and his lips were a thin line across his face.

The dancing finished there and then. There was a general disapproval in the air, and I could not but feel that my behaviour had been reprehensible. Miss Carteret, in particular, made her displeasure clear by leaving the room. Sir Leach looked positively shocked, whereas Lord Ebrington had a hint of lewdness in his eyes. Only Lady Dalrymple, Lord Elliot and Miss Elliot, who were busy finishing a game of pontoon, seemed unconcerned with what had just happened in front of them.

With the *sang froide* he must have shown a hundred times in the battlefield, Colonel Fitzwilliam diverted some of the attention by asking the Miss Bennets to sing for us. Regaining her composure, Lady Catherine suggested a game of pool, and a large group of guests was soon engrossed at the card table.

I was still in a haze. I needed a bit of solitude and fresh air to recollect myself. I went towards the balcony and stood there, the cold night air refreshing my temples. The thick curtains were hiding me from view, and I could feel the solid stone of the balcony under my gloved fingers. Alone, I would find peace.

Male steps came in my direction. Before I could make my presence known I heard the voice of Captain Price, darker than usual.

"Lowry, what we have just witnessed and what you told me the other night seems all designed with the sole purpose of tormenting me."

I kept still, enveloped by damask. They had not seen me, and I did not dare breathe.

"Never mind. There's plenty more fish in the sea, Price."

"Not like her. When our paths crossed for the first time, I thought I could see in her eyes the reflection of a soft and unprejudiced heart. How wrong I was."

"Forget her. There are many other ladies who will have you, and you won't have to go far, my dear fellow."

Captain Lowry gave a hollow laugh.

"It's not a good time to jest, Lowry. Oh, what's the use anyway? We are advised to find a match that benefits our wealth and connections. But what sane person would want to forsake genuine affection for the higher love of position or money?"

"Many do."

"Well, I will never marry to enlarge my fortune. I will marry for love."

"If you're foolish enough to do so, I'm sure you won't have trouble finding a suitable companion. There's at least one I can think of, and she's right there."

I could picture Captain Lowry pointing towards the drawing

room, where Kitty was still singing in a soft but pretty voice, a much better voice in any case than her sister's.

Captain Price sighed.

"If only I could go back to my teenage years and ask Margaret Kerr to marry me," he added after a short silence. "As a girl, she used to live in our street in Portsmouth. She had freckles and was fond of frogs. Alas, it's too late now: I last saw her two summers ago. She was married to a fisherman, had a brood of five and the figure to show for it."

Captain Price's companion laughed again.

"So what will you do, Price?"

"I fear that I am destined to be a lone wolf, one that wanders the forests when everyone is asleep, howling at the moon and longing for a mate."

"And I very much doubt that will be your destiny. I bet you five guineas that you will be a married man come Midsummer."

The voices of the two men retreated, their steps taking them away from the window.

My stomach was in a hard knot that I wasn't sure would ever untie.

* * *

When all guests had taken leave, my aunt sent my cousin away with an imperious gesture and made me sit across from her.

"Georgiana, you must tell me everything. Has Don Cosimo

asked you to marry him yet?"

I coloured deeply, then shook my head.

"No, Aunt, he has not."

"Oh."

It was the sound of disappointment, but she quickly recovered.

"Of course, you barely had any time together this evening. Alone, I mean. But with the waltzing, he has got as close to a public declaration of love as one might imagine. Yes, he has positioned himself as the most serious of your suitors. Has he been more specific to you in private?"

I felt panic rise in my chest.

The letters. I could never bring myself to admit their existence to my aunt, so after some hesitation, I shook my head again.

Lady Catherine's laughter made blood freeze in my veins. She grabbed my hand.

"You think I don't know about his correspondence?" she whispered. "Do not be a silly girl. I want to know exactly what he has said to you. Your cousin, if he is what worries you, is out of earshot."

There was no way out. I confessed to my aunt everything about Don Cosimo's letters, and even my secret outings to meet him. To my surprise, she did not get angry, and instead, she conspiratorially tapped my arm with her fan.

"Go to bed now. Lady Dalrymple's ball is on Friday. It will

all happen there."

Chapter 14

Two days later I was engaged to return my visit to Mrs Gardiner and the Misses Bennet at their Cheapside residence. Lady Catherine did not even contemplate the possibility of going herself. However, Colonel Fitzwilliam insisted in escorting me, and at the time agreed, a footman ushered us to the drawing room of the house, where Mr and Mrs Gardiner and their two nieces were awaiting us.

Mr Gardiner, perhaps eager for male company now he was living with three ladies, seemed to be particularly happy to see the Colonel, with whom he had coincided on occasion at Pemberley. Judging by their blushes and occasional glances, the Colonel was also a favourite with Mary and Kitty. Mrs Gardiner was as pleasant as ever and all was set for an agreeable visit, so I willed myself to feel at ease and enjoy the occasion.

The initial conversation centered on Lady Catherine's dinner.

There was a general agreement amongst our hosts that it had been the most elegant event they remembered attending, and that the guests were the most charming, eloquent and well-bred in the whole of London. My waltz with Don Cosimo was brushed under the carpet by the Gardiners, and I forced myself to ignore the odd glances coming from the Bennet girls and my cousin's stony silence on the matter.

The discussion quickly moved on to Mrs Darcy. I had received a letter from Mrs Bingley two days before, where she assured me that Elizabeth had recovered some vitality and was looking forward to the birth of the baby, which now was imminent.

Mr and Mrs Gardiner exchanged a look of worry. I shared their feelings. As my motherless state reminded me every day, giving birth was a serious business, and even mothers who had an easy labour with a happy outcome the first time were at risk of complications.

"But we were already informed of those particulars, Miss Darcy," interrupted Mary. "Jane also writes to us, you know. Don't you have a more recent letter?"

I blushed. I never thought Mary very clever, but her lack of manners was quite shocking. Granted, she spent most of her time alone with her parents these days, and her stay with the Gardiners was but a rare opportunity for her to leave Longbourn. But still, her comment was quite out of place. Mrs Gardiner quickly intervened.

"It is so comforting to know that Mrs Darcy has the company of her eldest sister. They have always provided each other with the utmost support, even in the most difficult of circumstances. Wouldn't you agree, Mr Gardiner?"

Mr Gardiner nodded and was going to add something else when he was interrupted by the footman, who discreetly entered the room and whispered something in his ear. Mr Gardiner's eyebrows jumped up, like caterpillars waking up and stretching their fuzzy bodies.

"What a surprise!" he exclaimed. "It would appear that Mrs Wickham has decided to pay us a visit, dear. She is waiting in the parlour."

"Lydia?"

My whole body tensed up, like a hound before the hunt. Across from me, Mrs Gardiner's regular features appeared disjointed for a few seconds, but she quickly recovered her composure. She then addressed the Colonel and me.

"Colonel Fitzwilliam, Miss Darcy, would you mind if my niece joined us?"

"Of course not, Mrs Gardiner. It will be a pleasure to see Mrs Wickham."

I looked at my cousin with some reticence. Ever the gentleman, he was as aware as I was that it would have been unthinkable to refuse, but there was no need to appear quite so willing.

As for me, I could feel my heart beat through the thin muslin of my dress. My enemy was sneaking into what I believed to be a safe place. I was like a crusader before going into combat, my eyes set on the gilded handle of the drawing room door.

A few moments later, Mrs Wickham entered with the confident step of a woman who knows herself to be alluring. She was looking rather lovely. Her hair was arranged in the latest fashion, and she was wearing a deep blue gown that I recognised immediately as one of Elizabeth's. As always in her presence, I became the clumsy goose placed next to a slinky cat. She joined the conversation with her usual eagerness to share her thoughts on everything. Clearly delighted to see my cousin, she flirted outrageously with him, asking him about the London entertainments he had enjoyed of late and repeatedly touching his sleeve, just as she had done a few weeks before at Pemberley.

Colonel Fitzwilliam was clearly enjoying the attention. Mr and Mrs Gardiner seemed somewhat uncomfortable, whereas Kitty was so entranced in observation of her younger sister that one might have said she was taking mental notes of her every move. Meanwhile, Mary had crossed her arms and legs and was looking out of the window.

Then, out of nowhere, Lydia addressed me.

"So, Miss Darcy, do you have many *beaux*, now you have been in town for a while?"

"I wouldn't say so, Mrs Wickham."

I tried to retreat, but she wouldn't let me. I was the helpless mouse, she the hungry feline.

"Come, you *must*! You are a rich heiress, and you were presented at court over a week ago! If my fortune had been but half of yours, I would have found myself a *Duke* in that time."

Kitty stifled a laugh, and Colonel Fitzwilliam smiled against his better judgement. I tried to appear calm but was seething inside. Thankfully, Mrs Gardiner stepped in.

"It is very wise of Miss Darcy not to state her preferences until it is safe for her to publicly declare her affections. Discretion should be paramount in such matters until there is the backing of a formal engagement. The kind of flattery and empty promises that so many young people enjoy these days are quite a waste of time."

"But they can be *delicious* too, Aunt! I must confess to having been subjected to a rather large dose of it of late."

Mrs Wickham had spoken with a mischievous look on her face. I was shocked. We all knew that Lydia was a flirt, but to articulate those words was unthinkable, even in an intimate gathering such as ours. She was a married woman.

Kitty fell for her sister's trap.

"Do you have an admirer, Lydia? Tell us more!"

"I do, and not just anyone. He is a titled nobleman, and lives in the most beautiful palace, coveted by the Pope himself."

At those words, my heart pounded faster, my stomach churned.

"I met him shortly after arriving in London, at a social gathering I was attending with my friend Mrs Slater," Lydia continued. "I was sitting down, just minding my own business, when he noticed my presence, came towards me and, with no hesitation, asked me to dance."

"Was Mr Wickham absent at the time?" Mrs Gardiner asked somewhat pointedly.

Lydia waved her hand as if a fly was bothering her.

"He was away with his regiment. Some exercise or other. But Wickham is the most understanding of husbands and doesn't expect me to stay at home, awaiting his return, with no friends or amusement. Anyway, this member of the *nobility* and I have danced together a great deal since. He is a very gifted waltz dancer."

Her eyes looked at me with intent. I shuddered. It couldn't be.

"He is *very* generous and buys me all sorts of jewellery and trinkets, which I always try to refuse to no avail. He is rather in love with me and assures me that he has never in his life admired a woman as much as he admires me. Alas, he says he is also rather desolate at my being married, but I think this only excites him further."

Mrs Gardiner was looking at her niece with alarm. Mr Gardiner seemed less shocked, but perhaps it was due to his male perspective, or the fact that past events had alerted him of the nature of his sister's youngest daughter. Colonel Fitzwilliam's smile was now a grimace, his eyebrows raised, but Kitty couldn't help herself.

"An aristocrat who gifts you jewels! How exciting! Do tell us, Lydia, is he handsome?"

"I do declare him to be. He has an *exceptionally* pleasing

countenance and the finest pair of eyes you ever saw in a man, although if you desire an impartial opinion, Miss Darcy here knows him well enough."

The floor disappeared from under my feet. I took a deep breath, willing to remain calm, but before I could say anything Lydia was speaking again.

"Come to think of it, you all know him! I believe that he was at Lady Catherine de Bourgh's the other night. Surely you remember Don Cosimo Giovanni Ludovico, Prince of Rasiglia and Ponziano?"

The surprise turned into horror. Mrs Gardiner gasped. I glanced in the direction of my cousin. His face was drained of colour; his fists turned into balls; his knuckles white. As for me, my cheeks reddened with painful shame. Lydia had exposed me as the worst of fools, for not only had I allowed a gentleman to claim my affections in public, but he had wronged me the whole time by having a favourite in the woman I most despised on earth.

I thought of the secret conversations Lydia and Don Cosimo must have had about me, their laughs and mockery at my expense. Was their amusement behind his letters? Was she helping him pen them without my knowledge? How could I have been so stupid? I lowered my gaze, unable to meet anyone's eyes, much less my cousin's, but Mrs Wickham had not finished.

"And guess what, Kitty? Miss Darcy is also well acquainted with your *beau*," she purred.

Kitty perked up, ecstatic to share the centre of attention with her sister.

"Do you mean Lieutenant Murphy? He is dreamy!"

"Don't be silly, Kitty! It's Captain Price I'm taking about. He admires you greatly. Remember how he was looking at you when we met him for the first time? A little bird has also told me that the other night at Lady Catherine's he was by your side the whole time. He only danced with you, did he not?"

Kitty hesitated, then nodded, and Lydia gave her a gleaming smile.

"Be in no doubt, Captain Price's affection for you is growing every day. I would not be surprised if he proposed before the end of the week."

I looked at Kitty, who seemed to be processing the information that Lydia had just given her. Kitty wasn't as accomplished as Jane and Elizabeth, but she had the pretty face, petite frame and graceful demeanour of the Bennet sisters, and a sweet air of innocence that Lydia lacked. As the second youngest daughter of Mr Bennet, she had little to recommend her in terms of dowry. However, she was connected to one of the most respectable families in the land: mine. She was perfect for a captain with a modest fortune, and, judging from his behaviour the previous night, Captain Price was well aware of it.

I lowered my head. Not for the first time, my wealth felt like an unshakeable burden that tied me to a gilded cage from which I would never escape. My distress must have been obvious to everyone, because Mr and Mrs Gardiner tried to defuse the tension, her engaging the ladies with light-hearted talk about new fashions and hairstyles, him introducing the subject of fishing to Colonel Fitzwilliam, but I'm ashamed to say that I never managed to compose myself. We left soon afterwards, the Colonel's hand protectively on my arm, not a single word passing his lips. I had never been so ashamed and wished I could scrub myself clean of the looks of pity of everyone in the room, save for Mrs Wickham, whose mocking smile never left her lips.

* * *

When we arrived at Grosvenor Square, my cousin went swiftly to the main drawing room while I excused myself. I needed some privacy to reflect on the events of the morning. I had long suspected Don Cosimo to be a particular favourite of the ladies, but that he should admire Mrs Wickham was a bitter pill to swallow. And so fervently, too! Lydia had a luminous beauty, a grace particularly becoming when dancing, and the large dark eyes of her oldest sister, but she was also inconsiderate, selfish and vain.

She may be, but so is her lover. And so is her husband, who almost disgraced you. Have you forgotten?

It was painful to acknowledge, but Don Cosimo had lied to me, just as Wickham had wronged me all those years back. It was a pattern that I was permitting. I had given them the power to make a fool out of me.

Tears started pouring down my eyes. The world was a blur,

but there was only one thing to do. I opened the trunk at the foot of the bed and fumbled around, looking for the ominous letters that had brought me such misery. I found them straight away, tied with a pink ribbon that I had removed from an old bonnet, and caught the sandalwood scent that perfumed their pages. My face burned at the thought of my past blunders, but soon the papers too were burning in the fireplace. It was futile, of course, but the sight of the flames devouring the words that had woven such a web of deception around my affections gave me some consolation.

My heart was broken once again, trampled on like an old doormat, but it wasn't only because of what I had learnt about Don Cosimo. Lydia's assurances about Captain Price's admiration for Kitty had been just as bad. I closed my eyes and saw the Captain for what I knew him to be: a good man, an excellent man, a man who represented all that was kind and fair in this world. From what I had seen and secretly witnessed at my aunt's, he was also eager to marry, and it was evident that Kitty had taken his fancy. Lydia was probably right. He surely was on the verge of proposing.

I must have fallen asleep.

There was a knock on my door. It was Jones, wanting to know if I needed any help preparing for that evening's outing. I had forgotten that we were due to attend a concert with Lady Dalrymple. I asked Jones to tell my aunt that I was feeling unwell, hoping to be left in peace so as to wallow in my misery, but shortly afterwards I heard footsteps go up the stairs and stop in front of my bedchamber door. After some whispering, Jones entered the room followed by Lady Catherine.

My aunt approached me in silence, observing in my swollen eyelids, tear-stained cheeks and crumpled dress. Taking my face in her hand, she looked into my eyes.

"Your cousin has explained everything to me. That Wickham woman is as vicious as her sister. I mourn the day that family crossed paths with ours."

I shrugged. I didn't have the energy to defend Elizabeth. Lady Catherine continued with bitterness in her voice, her fingers squeezing my cheeks.

"There is also Lady Hamilton, of course. She is spreading all sorts of gossip about that foreigner and you in town. I should have been on my guard. She was always a wicked woman. But no matter."

My aunt let go of my face and with determination folded her hands on her lap.

"Georgiana, you have the pride of the Darcys, but the resilience of the Fitzwilliams. You will rise above your shame in triumph. And you must look your best tonight."

I let out a cry, like an injured animal. I did not want to go anywhere. Ignoring my pleas, Lady Catherine's words became more urgent.

"We have lost the interest of Sir Leach and Lord Ebrington, who saw you waltz with the prince, but there are thousands of eligible single men in London. Only a handful will have been made aware of your dance the other night, and even less of them will know that you and your family have been fooled. We have to act quickly, before the story spreads."

Her eyes were glinting. I realised that marrying me to the best possible match was her mission, would perhaps be her last achievement in society, and that nothing would stop her. Not even me.

"You have to be at the Dalrymple box tonight, loooking your best, for everyone to see. Wear your white damask gown, and my diamonds, and the rubies as well, and the brooch you bought upon arriving in London. I will send Cosette up to help you. Your cousin and I will meet you downstairs in an hour."

I had no other option but to give in to her wishes, and nodded.

Chapter 15

As we were headed for the concert hall, I pulled my shawl around me. It was a mild evening, but the events of the day had chilled my very core. Colonel Fitzwilliam, who was sitting right across from me on the barouche, patted my hand, but I couldn't bring myself to look at him. His behaviour was completely altered. He was not only attentive to every single move I made, but he seemed to have also taken Don Cosimo's offence as his own.

Although we arrived early, the concert hall was already very busy. My cousin discreetly led us up to Lady Dalrymple's box, which was most conveniently situated and afforded a comprehensive view of the stage and the audience. I was terrified of hearing any comments about the waltz I had danced with Don Cosimo from our hosts, but I shouldn't have worried. Miss Carteret only reaction was to look at me with disdain in her eyes and snigger. As for Lady Dalrymple, she seemed utterly unfazed about it, and even mentioned the gentleman in question to say that, although he had been invited to join the Dalrymple box, he had declined on account of a prior engagement. Relief invaded my body; at least I would not see Don Cosimo tonight. As soon as it was polite to do so I sank into my crimson velvet seat, wishing to become invisible.

The concert began shortly afterwards. The music was heavenly and it enveloped me quickly, dissolving my despair and shame into thin air. The first half flew by, and before I knew it, the interval arrived. Lady Dalrymple found the concert hall too crowded and insisted that we should all stay in the box, but my aunt had other plans.

"The Earl of Broughton, who is seated in a box to our right, has been trying to catch your eye for the last half hour," she whispered in my ear. "I believe you made *quite* an impression on him at Almack's. He looks about to leave his box at this very moment. You must meet him in the corridor or downstairs. The Colonel will escort you. Now, go!"

I was terrified of running into anyone who might laugh at my naiveté with regards to Don Cosimo, but I was much more afraid of my aunt's anger if I refused to obey her instructions, so I did as she wanted. Soon afterwards, I was on the arm of the Colonel, and he was leading me down the stairs.

The interval had brought a large number of the audience to the refreshment rooms. Beneath the large chandeliers and gold leaf arches, the crowd moved and buzzed like insects in an eating frenzy. Colonel Fitzwilliam was my shield against strangers, but even for him, reaching the tables where tea was being served was unfeasible. I quickly realised that I would never in a million years find the earl amongst the crowd, and was about to suggest to my cousin that we go back to the box when we ran into the Wentworths and Captain Price.

Captain Wentworth was genial as usual. He seemed happy to see us and was too much of a gentleman to even hint at the snub he and his wife had been a subject of at Lady Catherine's. Captain Price was smiling, but not in his usual frank manner.

"Miss Darcy, you are as bright as the chandelier above us tonight," he said to me. "Those stones are magnificent."

"My aunt insisted that I should wear them. They are hers."

"Surely you will have a closet full of diamonds at Pemberley?"

I blushed.

"I don't, Captain. As a matter of fact, I care little for jewellery."

"So you say, Miss Darcy, but I bet that's not the case."

His tone was teasing, as if it was all a harmless joke, but I knew better. His blue eyes were clouded. He was testing me. At that moment, Mrs Wentworth joined our conversation.

"Ah, Mrs Wentworth. Miss Darcy and I were discussing treasured possessions. What are yours, I wonder?"

"I am not much attached to things, Captain. I much prefer

people. But I keep a letter from my husband that is very dear to me."

She looked up towards Captain Wentworth with deep affection. He seemed to notice her gaze and immediately smiled in her direction. I wondered if I would ever get to experience something akin to the love that Captain Wentworth and his wife felt for each other.

"I don't imagine we will ever get to read it," replied Captain Price playfully, "although I must admit I am curious as to its content, given that you rate it dearer to you than the diamond earrings he bought you for your birthday."

Mrs Wentworth let out a clear laugh.

"I am sorry! I forgot that you helped him pick them."

"I wouldn't say as much, Mrs Wentworth. I was more like a mute witness to his decision making. Captain Wentworth has excellent taste, as you well know."

"No doubt, he will be delighted to hear that you have downplayed your contribution. But it is your turn. What objects do you treasure the most, Captain?"

Captain Price immediately looked at me.

"Us sailors are uncomplicated. Our life on board gives us but limited room for our wares, and we grow used to living with little. However, there is a particular item that I am rather attached to: a silver hip flask that was a present from my dear sister Fanny."

Guilt enveloped me.

"Unfortunately the hip flask is no longer in my possession," he continued. "I gave it to a friend who subsequently promised to return it to me, and has failed to do so. As a result, I am forced to believe that this particular person is perhaps much less thoughtful and considerate than I initially believed."

"Those are harsh words, Captain," said Mrs Wentworth's in a gentle tone. "Surely your friend has not found the occasion."

"Oh, there have been many opportunities, Mrs Wentworth, believe me. Perhaps I am seen as too lowly, and hence not worthy of attention."

His words were like daggers. My eyes tingled, but the Fitzwilliam spirit my aunt had called upon earlier came to my rescue. I took a deep breath.

"I, too, have a favourite possession, Captain Price," I said in a steady voice.

"Of course you do, Miss Darcy. Which one of your many precious treasures is it? Is it this jewel-encrusted brooch, perchance?"

Mrs Wentworth looked mildly alarmed by the Captain's hostile tone. With all the dignity I could muster, and unable to stop the tears from appearing in my eyes, I replied,

"My most cherished possession is the miniature of my mother that my father had made when I was not yet born. It was her last portrait before she died at my birth."

The Captain's expression turned from mockery to shame, and he lowered his gaze.

The first bell announcing the end of the intermission rang.

There were rushed ends to conversations, hushed voices, laughter. The crowd began to move towards the concert hall, and us with it. Colonel Fitzwilliam was walking ahead of us, with Captain Wentworth by his side. Mrs Wentworth, Captain Price and I followed behind.

Then I saw him.

Wickham was standing by one of the windows, watching me. When he was sure I had caught his eye, he came in my direction. His figure was wearier, less elegant than I remembered, and I quickly detected a limp. As he got closer, I also noticed his thinning hair, his red and swollen nose, and above all, the change in his eyes. Once lively and full of mischief, and so dear to me, they were now bloodshot, with a yellow tinge that denoted ill health.

I felt panic rise inside of me and I looked around for my cousin. I cried his name, but my voice was swallowed up by the noise of the crowd. Wickham was now right in front of me. I thought my legs would fail me, but Captain Price, who had kept to my side upon noticing that I was agitated, was holding my arm, his firm grip steadying me.

With a smirk that showed a gap where one of his incisors should have been, Wickham gave me an exaggerated bow.

"Dearest Georgiana, what a pleasure to see you after all these years."

Before we could continue, a shrill female voice cried.

"Captain Price, what a surprise!"

Lydia.

She practically ran towards us, her low-cut gown barely able to contain her bosom. Oblivious to any tension in the air, she proudly introduced Captain Price to her husband, who gave him a hostile smile. The Captain's face I could not see, but I noticed the muscles in his body tense up.

"Kitty will be *so* disappointed to have missed you when I tell her that I saw you tonight," Mrs Wickham added.

Captain Price mumbled some formulaic form of regret, but Lydia insisted.

"My sister is *quite* taken with you, Captain, and I dare venture that the feeling is mutual. Oh, come, do not pretend it isn't, you are amongst friends! But do not despair, you do not have long to wait until you speak to her again. You will see her at Lady Dalrymple's ball tomorrow. Did you know I'm going as well?"

All the while, Wickham was watching me like a hungry tiger, completely ignoring his wife. Had I been alone, I would have been easy pray for him, but the Captain's arm gave me strength. Lydia didn't seem to mind his behaviour, and continued her monologue as if the conversation was perfectly pleasant for all present.

"And Miss Darcy is here as well, Wickham, just as you said! How did you know?"

Her words came as no surprise to me. I could easily picture Wickham carefully planning the encounter, hoping that I would be left without a protector in a moment of confusion. I began to tremble, I thought I would surely faint, but the Captain had me, and I held on to him as if I was a shipwreck survivor and he the only floating piece of wood in the ocean. Captain Price immediately excused us with perfect manners and the pretext that the performance was recommencing, and he steered me towards the stairs. As we were leaving, I could feel Wickham's gaze still on me, with a mixture of glee, anger and something deeper and more disturbing I couldn't quite place.

When we were out of the Wickham's view, Captain Price made me stop.

"Miss Darcy, you are unwell," he said in a hushed voice, his blue eyes tinged with worry. "Allow me to find you a seat, and fetch you a glass of cordial to restore your spirits."

"No!"

In my agitation, I buried my head in his shoulder.

For a split second, I feared he would tease me about my distress, but he didn't say a word, and we remained standing in the corridor until the musicians started playing again. When I finally plucked the courage to look up at him, there was concern in his clear blue eyes, but above all kindness.

"I promise I will not leave you, Miss Darcy," he said in a solemn voice, offering me his handkerchief. "I will remain by your side as long as you desire."

The words were the balm my heart needed. I wiped away the tears from my face, took a deep breath and willed myself to recover my self-command. I was suddenly embarrassed and began to apologise, but the Captain wouldn't hear of it.

"It is I, Miss Darcy, who should apologise for my earlier behaviour. My snares were uncivil and rude, and most unjustly aimed. I am so very sorry I ever caused you pain."

At that moment, Colonel Fitzwilliam appeared, a look of concern on his face. He saw us, the handkerchief, the tears.

"What is the matter, Georgiana?" he asked, giving Captain Price a most severe look.

I couldn't have the man who had now twice come to my assistance be unjustly seen as the cause of my misery, so I forced myself to speak in spite of the shock I was feeling.

"I was in some distress," I said in a whisper, "and Captain Price came to my assistance."

My cousin's eyes narrowed.

Captain Price kept his gaze on Colonel Fitzwilliam and addressed him with perfect calmness and collection.

"I am afraid that Miss Darcy's spirits have been sorely tested. She needs a rest. If she so wishes, I will fetch her shawl from your box so you can take her home."

The Captain looked at me, and I nodded, and with that, he departed. When I was sure only my cousin could hear me, I spoke to him in a low voice.

"I saw Wickham. He was downstairs."

Colonel Fitzwilliam stiffened, his lips tweaked for an instant, and his face reddened. He started to ask me questions, but I did not find the energy to answer, and simply let him pat my hands, just as he would pat one of his hounds to calm her down. Captain Price was at our side in an instant and he put the shawl around my shoulders. He had informed Lady Catherine that I had suddenly taken ill and that the Colonel would escort me back to Grosvenor Square. A moment later, my cousin and I were in the carriage and Captain Price had waved me goodbye.

Colonel Fitzwilliam was bitter and deeply troubled all the way back to my aunt's house.

"Wickham would not have dared to address you directly, or even make his presence known, had I been with you. I will never forgive myself for not having prevented this encounter, Georgiana. I am sorrier than I can express."

I wanted to assuage his feelings but I truly couldn't. I was too agitated to try to calm another.

A half hour later, alone in bed, my temples tingling due to the lavender water that Jones had most expediently applied at the sight of my pale face, the events repeated themselves behind my closed eyes.

It had been shocking to see Wickham, but also enlightening. Reality had brusquely shown me that the man I had thought him to be was a figment of my imagination. My memories of Wickham, his handsome looks, his graceful countenance, his spellbinding conversation, these all remained, but they were forever tainted by the recent sighting of the person he had become. The final scraps of chivalry and dignity he still had when I met him last had been lost forever. Best of all, the weight that had been oppressing me since that day in Ramsgate had finally lifted. I was finally free from him.

* * *

In the small hours, when the streets were as silent as they get in London, I went towards the window and drew the curtains back, allowing the moonlight to flood the room. Carefully, I opened the trunk at the foot of the bed for the second time that day. After some rummaging, my fingers struck metal, and I took out Captain Price's hip flask. I held the silver item in my hands, feeling its weight, its rounded edges, its scratches and imperfections due to years of travel and service in the Navy. It was flawed but dignified and beautiful at the same time.

It was time to return it to its rightful owner.

I hid the hip flask in the reticule I was planning to take to Lady Dalrymple's ball. I would see him there, and even if he was busy dancing with Kitty Bennet, I was sure to find a moment with him. Satisfied with my decision, I closed the curtains and tiptoed back to bed.

Chapter 16

On the morning of Lady Dalrymple's ball, the sun was out, and for once the London streets didn't seem so bleak. I eagerly jumped out of bed and went straight to the wardrobe. My new blue gown was hanging inside, the beautiful silk soft and shiny, the lace and ribbons perfectly ironed and ready for tonight's entertainments. I checked the azure slippers I had bought in South Molton Street: they matched the rest of the attire perfectly. I reddened at the memory of the expedition with Mrs Gardiner and the Misses Bennet. I could not change the past, but today arrived with the opportunity to make amends. I dressed in my morning gown and went downstairs.

My aunt wasn't at the table. My cousin, who was finishing his meal, looked up from his eggs, his eyes tinged with concern.

"Good morning, Georgiana, I hope you have recovered from

last night."

I nodded.

"The encounter was unpleasant in the extreme, Cousin, but I am in better spirits today."

Colonel Fitzwilliam rested his knife and fork on the edge of his plate and put his hand on mine.

"I am happy to hear, Georgiana."

He seemed bewildered by my speedy recovery. Of course, he couldn't know that the encounter with Wickham had given me clarity. I may never be able to declare in public my affection for Captain Price, but I could return to him what was rightly his and keep his friendship in the bargain. A wave of anticipation was building inside of me. I would see him again in just a few hours.

The Colonel coughed.

"Unfortunately, I am afraid to report that the evening didn't agree with our aunt."

"What do you mean, Cousin?"

"Lady Catherine has taken to her bed. I have called for a doctor, and he should be here presently. Of course, her illness means that we will not be able to go to the ball tonight," he added in a matter-of-fact voice. "I have taken the liberty of writing to Lady Dalrymple and excusing us from attending."

"But –"

"I am sorry, Georgiana, but it would be improper to attend in the present circumstances."

My eyes tingled. There would be no ball for me after all. We both fell silent. I forced myself to eat, but I had no appetite. Then, the footman came into the breakfast room holding a silver tray. On it was an envelope addressed to my cousin. Colonel Fitzwilliam took it with a sharp gesture, slashed it open with his penknife and read the contents with impatience. His manner alarmed me.

"Is it from Pemberley, Cousin? I hope it's good news."

My cousin swiftly stood up, his face visibly pale.

"Apologies, Georgiana, but I have some urgent business to attend to."

And with that, he left. I had no inkling of the affairs he was involved in, but it all sounded very disturbing.

The rest of the day dragged on miserably. I tried to read a novel from my aunt's library, but I didn't manage to get beyond page fifteen. I picked up my sewing box but was unable to do concentrate. All I could think of was the dancing and falling in love that would happen between Captain Price and Kitty, all of it away from my gaze. For some reason, imagining the events instead of witnessing them seemed infinitely worse. Furthermore, there was the hip flask. My plans to return it had been shattered. I was feeling utterly miserable.

* * *

In the afternoon, the doorbell rang, and to my surprise the footman announced Mrs Wentworth. She came in, dressed in a green cotton gown that brought out the hazel in her eyes. She smiled at me gently as if she needed to excuse her presence.

"I happened to be at Lady Dalrymple's with my father and sister when your aunt's footman brought the Colonel's note excusing you all from tonight's ball. I did not wish to intrude, but I imagined that you may welcome some company."

I was delighted to see her. There was a gentleness, a caring nature in her that, although entirely different from Elizabeth's, was missing in my life since my departure from Pemberley. I asked the maid to bring some tea. While it was being served, Mrs Wentworth handed me a card.

"I also wanted to invite your party to a gathering the Captain and I are hosting at our residence in Cavendish Square Gardens on Saturday night. It will be a much less grand affair than Lady Dalrymple's ball, but I thought perhaps you would appreciate the chance to be out in society, even if your aunt is unable to accompany you. Surely Colonel Fitzwilliam will do the honours."

I assented with some reserve. I would have to speak to him first. These days I no longer knew what was possible and what wasn't.

"I must enquire after Lady Catherine," continued Mrs Wentworth. "How is she?"

"She is in her rooms, in need of rest. I fear that she has been overexerting herself since I arrived in London."

My voice was faltering. Mrs Wentworth gently pressed my hand.

"Do not blame yourself. Lady Catherine has an enviable

constitution for someone her age, and she will recover. And as for the ball, I know it is of little consolation to you, but there will be many more such nights. In London, there is always something happening, and you would be surprised at how often one encounters the same familiar faces over and over again."

She meant Don Cosimo, of course. The gossip on his deception had not yet reached her, and she thought me in love with him. I had an overwhelming urge to explain it to her myself, to say how wrong I had been, how little I cared for him now, and how my affections had a much more worthy recipient, even if I dared not dream of a future with him. But I couldn't. My sense of pride and duty, mixed with my natural timidity, made the disclosure impossible, even to such an amiable ear. Mrs Wentworth seemed to acknowledge that there was a fight of some description taking place inside of me, but her discreet manner prevailed.

I suddenly realised that I would not see Captain Price tonight, but she surely would. I must give her the hip flask. It was the only way to convey to him the message that I was thinking about him. I stood up in haste.

"Mrs Wentworth, would you be able to wait here for five minutes?"

She assented, slightly confused.

I rushed upstairs and fetched the reticule that I would not need that night. Back in the drawing room, I opened it and extracted the hip flask, which was folded in one of my embroidered handkerchiefs.

"Would you do me a great favour and hand this back to its rightful owner, Captain Price?" I asked Mrs Wentworth, placing the object in her hands.

She looked at the hip flask and then at me with wide eyes. She did not ask, but I felt compelled to explain to her how the object had come to my possession.

"Captain Price came to my assistance when I needed it most, and was generous enough to leave this hip flask with me at the time. I have been meaning to return it to him for some time, and had finally settled in doing so at Lady Dalrymple's tonight. However, it won't be possible, and hence my appeal for your help. I know I can trust your delicacy and discretion."

Silently, she took the object and put it in her reticule.

"I may have been surprised to hear your story if it had involved anyone else but Captain Price," she said after some reflection. "He possesses a kind heart and the determination and courage to assist those in need. My husband told me that, a few days ago, upon seeing a bunch of street urchins wearing Navy gear, Captain Price didn't satisfy himself with giving them generous alms. He spoke to them, found out that their departed father once served under an acquaintance and is now determined to raise funds to assist them."

It couldn't be the same children I had spotted from my carriage, surely? I remembered the frantic obstinacy of the eldest child, the cloudy and useless eyes of the toddler, and prayed it was indeed them.

"Captain Wentworth thinks very highly of his friend," continued Mrs Wentworth. "He often says that Captain Price is the bravest and most loyal of his colleagues, but more importantly, a good man, and that if only there were more people like him in the world, it would surely be a better place."

My thoughts exactly. Her words sent a warm wave all over my body.

Mrs Wentworth left shortly afterwards. Her slight figure entered her landaulette with a graceful movement, the heavy reticule giving away its contents. I went towards the table where tea had been served and took the invite she had handed me earlier. It was a beacon in what had so far been a rather dark day.

* * *

I hardly slept that night. The odd noises coming from nearby streets, which had given me no cause for complaint until that moment, now seemed unbearable. My pillow felt too warm, and I tossed and turned in my bed, then got out and paced up and down my room with the anguish of those who feel left out. I didn't want to think about Kitty and the Captain, but inevitably I did, and suffered in doing so. I finally gave into slumber in the small hours, and was grateful when I finally opened my eyes to the morning sun.

It was late, but my cousin was still at the breakfast table. He had been reading the newspaper, but he must have folded it as soon as he heard me come down the stairs. I murmured a good morning, and he surprised me by coming to greet me at the door.

"Dear Georgiana, I couldn't help but hear you last night. Are you indisposed?"

"It was nothing."

"But I see that you haven't rested well."

For a fleeting moment, cousin Fitzwilliam took my chin with his index finger and lifted my face towards him, fixing his eyes tenderly on me. The gesture was so out of place that I dropped the book that I had brought downstairs and was planning to read later in the parlour.

"Allow me," he said, bending down to retrieve it for me.

With a gallant ceremony which I had witnessed in the past but never been the recipient of, my cousin ushered me to my seat. He then proceeded to watch me eat with an expression that I couldn't quite place. It wasn't concern, but rather more like extreme interest. To defuse his attention, I enquired after my aunt.

"I saw Lady Catherine this morning," he explained. "She is in better spirits, but the doctor insists that she needs to rest some more. She has also asked after you, and wants to go up to her room for a visit later today. She will send her maid to fetch you."

"Of course."

"Speaking of visits, Dewars has told me that Mrs Wentworth came to enquire after our aunt's health yesterday afternoon and that she stayed for half an hour."

I nodded. I wasn't sure what my cousin was getting at.

"Mrs Wentworth is a sensible and entirely respectable woman. I have consulted with our aunt, and we have no objections to you becoming more acquainted with her. In fact, we would be quite happy to encourage it."

"That is uncanny, Cousin, because Mrs Wentworth also handed me an invitation for dinner on Saturday night. She sounded keen to see us there."

My cousin's features immediately darkened.

"I am afraid that accepting to attend a dinner party wouldn't be proper while Lady Catherine is unwell. She may take a while to recover, I fear. Her health hasn't been the same since suffering the loss of poor Cousin Anne, and the doctor has been quite clear. It is unlikely she'll be able to engage socially in the foreseeable future." My disappointment must have shown because he hastened to add, "Of course, I realise it would be rather cruel to condemn you to spend the rest of the season locked up in this house. Your brother said that Mrs Annesley is visiting family in Gloucestershire, but I will write to her and ask her to cut her stay short. We need her in London to keep you company."

I thought of my faithful companion for the last five years. Upon knowing that I was to travel to London to be with Lady Catherine for the best part of three months, she had jumped at the chance to visit her sister and spend some time with her twin nephews. Surely, it would be cruel to snatch her away from her loved ones so soon.

"I don't think that cutting Mrs Annesley's stay with her

family short will be necessary," I said. "I already have a few friends in London."

Cousin Fitzwilliam looked at me. His brow creased and his eyes softened.

"I suppose you do. But we must keep engagements to a minimum until Lady Catherine has recovered. Anyway, I expect there will be far less need for you to socialise, at least for the purposes our aunt initially had in mind."

With those words, he took my hand in his and kissed it again, and this time his whiskers lingered on my skin for longer than strictly necessary. Then he resolutely stood up.

"Now, I must write to your brother at once," he said in a strained voice.

He swiftly departed the breakfast room, leaving me with more questions than answers.

* * *

That afternoon, Mr and Mrs Collins stopped at Grosvenor Square for a short visit. My cousin had not returned, so I received them on my own. Mr Collins seemed visibly concerned.

"So it is true! Lady Catherine de Bourgh is affected by the gravest of maladies! I cannot express the dread I felt when your ladyship's footman informed us of the news. We were so very fortunate to run into him just outside Fortnum & Mason. You see, I was rather alarmed when I didn't see her at the Dowager

Viscountess Dalrymple's ball last night. Lady Catherine de Bourgh was so very kind to entreat the Dowager Viscountess Dalrymple to invite us. I know for a fact that she used her influence most generously on the hostess to ensure our names were added to the guest list in spite of our relatively humble station in life, at least while Mr Bennet is alive."

Mrs Collins coughed. I ignored his comment.

"Please do not feel alarmed, Mr Collins. My aunt is only temporarily indisposed."

"Oh, but to have such a great lady immersed in the evils of infirmity! Such a tender heart, such a generous and forgiving nature! We all owe her so much, even you, Miss Darcy, if I may say so. Her coming to London against her natural inclination to retire from this world after the bitter disappointments she has had to bear in the last few years was done just to ensure your happiness, so wouldn't it be atrocious if we lost her because of this last act of selflessness?"

It hadn't crossed my mind that I could remotely be the cause of my aunt's death, but it was evident that Mr Collins saw it as a viable reason for her demise.

"I am sure Miss Darcy understands the gravity of her situation and prays for her aunt's recovery as eagerly as you do," said Mrs Collins timidly. While her husband looked puzzled she continued, "Miss Darcy, you must have felt some disappointment at not being able to come to the ball last night. If we had known, it would have been an honour to accompany you."

Her husband didn't allow me to reply.

"But my dear Mrs Collins, I'm sure Miss Darcy didn't even think of the pleasures of dancing when her aunt was on the verge of meeting her Maker! Moreover, they were spared that ghastly incident. I shudder just to think that Lady Catherine de Bourgh's pious soul might have been forced to witness it."

"May I enquire as to what happened at the ball, Mr Collins?" I couldn't help but ask.

Mr Collins took a deep breath.

"I'm afraid I cannot *possibly* bring myself to describe what went on," he said, after a dramatic pause. "It was all too shocking to be discussed in polite company. Imagine, two gentlemen and a lady behaving like anything but! All in all, a shameful affair that ought to bring the utmost reprehension from all quarters of Christian society. My particular cross to bear is that a close connection of mine is the lady involved in this sordid matter, and hence my lips are sealed. I will not discuss anything further."

He stopped here, looking at me pointedly, his eyebrows raised. He clearly wanted me to insist and drag the unpleasant details out of him, but I didn't need to. The lady in question had to be Lydia Wickham, and I could guess the identity of the gentlemen. All at once I felt tired. I wanted to be left alone.

Mrs Collins, who was perceptive where Mr Collins was oblivious, immediately understood that I wished them to take leave, and gently steered her husband's conversation away from the previous night, to focus on the framed picture they were supposed to collect from town. Before leaving, Mr Collins insisted on the tragedy of Lady Catherine's imminent departure from this world and his wish that she should do so with little suffering. I repeated my assurances that the doctor trusted in my aunt's prompt recovery, but nevertheless, Mr Collins made me promise that I would send a servant to fetch him, should her end be nearer than anticipated.

When the door closed behind the Collins, I sat down on the couch and my aunt's lapdog, exiled from the sickroom, promptly jumped on my lap. As I was stroking its ears, one big question hovered over me: what exactly had Lydia done at Lady Dalrymple's ball that had so scandalised Mr Collins?

Chapter 17

Jones brought me the answer later that day, when she returned from running an errand in one of the shops around Oxford Street. Upon assessing my wardrobe that same morning, she had decided that the silk fabric covering a small section of my favourite fan needed replacing, and she had headed into town to get it mended. I suspected that the real reason behind her excursion was less diligent and revolved around the opportunity it gave her to find out more about the incident at Lady Dalrymple's ball the previous night, but I didn't complain. I was rather curious now as to what had exactly happened. She quickly obliged upon her return, as she was serving me a cup of tea.

"It's everywhere, ma'am. A big scandal. Turns out, last night Mrs Darcy's youngest sister, Mrs Wickham, ran into Don Cosimo at the ball. Apparently, it was plain for everyone to see they were friends right enough, if you get my drift, with looks and dancing and what have you in full view of all guests."

I couldn't help but blush upon recalling the web of lies that Don Cosimo had spun around me while he was flirting with Lydia behind my back. His letters, so charming and affectionate; our musical duet; our waltz that fateful evening under the eyes of so many people – they were all illusions. His affections were for another. I felt a mixture of embarrassment and indignation. How could a well-bred gentleman be capable of such evil concealment and scandalous behaviour? But Jones hadn't finished.

"Then, out of the blue, the doors opened and in came the husband! He walked into the ballroom with his pistol in his hand, ma'am, as if he was at Waterloo and not in one of the most elegant houses in London. He went straight for his wife and her lover, and there was a big palaver, so I'm told, with the lady screaming and having a fit and guests restraining the men. Your friends Captain Wentworth and Captain Price got the Wickham man to drop the weapon, or who knows what might have happened."

Jones was delighting in her storytelling, oblivious to my pallor.

"Things took a turn for the worse when the daughter of the hostess, Miss Carteret, threw herself at the feet of the Italian prince, crying and asking him why he was so cruel towards her. Mrs Wickham jumped on her straightaway, so they say, and they started pulling each other's hair and screaming down the house! The yelling got louder, with Mr Wickham accusing Don Cosimo of seducing his wife and then deceiving her, and what have you."

What Jones was retelling was extraordinary. I couldn't quite picture Miss Carteret humiliating herself so in public, but then I remembered her scathing looks every time Don Cosimo paid me any kind of attention, and realised that her contempt for me must have been hiding her fear of losing what little affection he had for her. Poor Miss Carteret, she must have been very much in love with him to behave in that manner.

With a dramatic gesture, Jones inclined herself towards me.

"People say there will be consequences," she whispered. "Apparently, the gentlemen have already arranged to meet at first light tomorrow morning on Primrose Hill."

"A duel? Never!"

"Oh, yes, ma'am. It's on everyone's lips. What with the husband being a soldier and the lover a nobleman, all bets point towards the same result. It's a bad business, ma'am. Very bad. For the family, too."

Jones' brow was creased, her mouth twisted. She knew as well as I that it would be difficult for the Darcy name to stay out of the newspapers if there was indeed a duel and one of the two men lost his life as a result. The Darcys of Pemberley dragged into another scandal by the lady's side of the family; it had been bad enough when Lydia had run away with Wickham. Now, it was much worse.

I thought of Don Cosimo's handsome features frozen in a mask of blood and death, his exquisitely embroidered white shirt stained red, his shapely lips forever parted. He had a soul as vain and selfish as that of his would-be killer, but it was a nonsensical way to die. And for a woman like Lydia too!

There was a knock on the door. It was Cosette, informing me that Lady Catherine was requesting my company presently. I recalled the memory of my last visit to Elizabeth's sickroom; this one would be very different, I had no doubt about it.

* * *

My aunt's maid opened the door for me in silence. The bedchamber was as ornate as the main drawing room, with delicate cornices and gilded detailing framing the silk-covered walls. The heavy purple curtains were only partially drawn, and it was much darker in there than in the parlour, so it took a few moments for my eyes to adjust and take everything in.

My aunt was lying in her grand French bed, which, according to family legend, had belonged to the Duchess of Polignac and had been dismantled piece by piece and sent across to England on the eve of Louis XVI's execution. Lady Catherine was wearing a white gown and bonnet and looked very pale against the creamy silk of the upholstered headboard. Her eyeslids were closed, and her skin had a waxy texture as if it had melted around her cheeks, jaw and mouth. Then I noticed the dentures sitting on her bedside table. Whether they were ivory or porcelain, I wasn't able to ascertain, but it was yet another reminder that my formidable aunt was getting old.

Lady Catherine opened one slate eye, then the other, and her corpse-like body slowly became alive, speaking with her usual frankness and a distorted voice that gave away her paucity of teeth.

"Georgiana, that dress doesn't suit your complexion at all in this light. You must banish it from your wardrobe."

Then, with a swift gesture, she grabbed the dentures and inserted them into her mouth. After some deft manoeuvring, she seemed satisfied with their positioning and continued her speech.

"I know that the Colonel has been keeping you up-to-date with everything concerning my temporary indisposition. I dare say you must find my ill health rather inconvenient and must be disappointed that your social life has been so severely curtailed."

I opened my mouth to protest, but she raised her hand.

"I do not blame you in the slightest, Georgiana. After all, the pleasures that London has to offer must be a refreshing change from the long years you have spent locked in Pemberley. However, I must confess that in my current state I feel rather relieved that I am too unwell to act as your chaperone. In spite of my best intentions, and given the recent events, I believe I do not have the nerves to take you on a tour of the city's best drawing rooms and balls in quest of a suitable husband."

"But Aunt –"

She looked at me with her famously penetrating eyes.

"Do not pretend that I do not know what I am talking about now. You must have heard about what happened last night, at Lady

Dalrymple's ball; your maid is not stupid, and the whole city is gossiping about it. Don Cosimo was a charming suitor and a desirable match, a man of consequence and fortune with the right kind of connections. But you should have been on your guard. That waltz was scandalous, especially for an unmarried young woman like you. Some may say I'm from a different generation, but if you knew he had no intention to propose, you should have never accepted to dance with him."

I blushed yet again at the recollection, and at my aunt's twisting of the events, but didn't say anything.

"In my time, noblemen also had their indiscretions, but it was all carried out most properly and out of sight, and they certainly did not deceive young ladies into thinking they were about to ask for their hands, at least not deliberately. It must be all that foreign blood of his. An Englishman would have never acted in that manner."

Lady Catherine was no longer looking at me. Her gaze was fixed on the patch of sky visible through the window hangings. In the dramatic light, she resembled an ancient tortoise who has seen everything in life. She turned in my direction, narrowed her eyes and her face turned into a grimace.

"Don Cosimo may have fooled us, but he is the greater fool. To lose so much for the love of that wanton woman! That she is related to the Darcys only makes it worse. I knew things would be bad when your brother took that Bennet girl as a wife, but even in my worst nightmares I could not have anticipated the dishonour that she would bring to our family."

My cheeks were burning with outrage at the insults addressed to someone so dear to me, but I dared not face my aunt's anger. I braced myself for more, but instead of further sullying my sister-in-law's name, Lady Catherine went quiet and looked pensive for few moments.

"Yes, Don Cosimo has sorely disappointed me. How different his behaviour is from that of your cousin. Colonel Fitzwilliam is so thoughtful and considerate. Did you know that after your brother was foolish enough to marry so beneath him, I contemplated him as a potential husband for poor dear Anne? She could have married anyone in England, but the more I reflected on their possible union, the more convinced I grew that it would be a perfectly suited match. What the Colonel lacks in fortune he makes up with his many personal charms, and Anne's sweet temper would have agreed with his affectionate disposition. Alas, she was very weak by then. It was never to be."

Lady Catherine took a delicate lace handkerchief from under her pillowcase and brought it to the corners of her eyes.

"Speaking of the Colonel, I might as well tell you that I have discussed you with him a few times in the last day or two, and he has shared some intelligence with me regarding some incident a few years back that has caused me no little pain. It has been so upsetting, in fact, that I would rather not allude to it. I am sure you know that which I refer to."

I felt my skin crawl and fought down the urge to scratch

myself until I bled. So she knew about my frustrated plans for elopement with Wickham. Cousin Fitzwilliam had betrayed my confidence, and my brother's as well. How dared he? I clenched my jaw, willed myself to keep silent and reveal nothing. My aunt ignored my agitation and continued to speak.

"This most sensitive information, however, has provided me with much greater insights into the workings of your mind. I for one see every inch of my sister in you. Granted, she was a renowned beauty and you are not, but you are just like her, a pleasure-seeking fool who basks in male attention. She was lucky to secure the affections of such an honourable man as your father so early in her first season, or I fear she might have been involved in a scandal and brought disgrace to the family."

Fury turned to sadness. I had never heard anyone speak of my mother in those terms. My eyes welled up and I bit the inside of my mouth to avoid the inevitable, but it was of little use, and soon tears were streaming down my cheeks.

Lady Catherine seemed to mellow a little when she saw me cry and gave me a little pat with her liver-spotted hand.

"Now, now, there are other ways to marry you off to a man of honour with wonderful family connections without risking your virtue. You are bright enough, and I am sure you will eventually come to understand the convenience of the arrangement to all parties involved, but for now, I must not say another word. I promised your cousin that I would not talk about it until your brother has been made aware of the situation. He will need to give his consent, of course, but that should not be a problem."

Her lips were pursed into what may or may not have been a smile. A gold spring was visible in the corner of her mouth. I shuddered inwardly but tried to betray no emotion. The plans of my aunt and my cousin were slowly becoming sharper, more defined, but I still could not face their implications. All I could think was that I wanted to wake up from the living nightmare I was experiencing, where every shred of self-determination was being taken away from me. I left my aunt and went up to my room to cry my heart out.

* * *

At dinner time, I was anxious to see that there was just Colonel Fitzwilliam and myself seated at the table. I timidly asked him if there had been any news from Pemberley, as I had not received any letters from my usual correspondents for three days now, but my cousin brushed my worries aside, mumbling that no news usually meant good news. Then, he brusquely changed the subject.

"I have to go to Brighton for a couple of nights. I will be back on Sunday."

His words shattered the little hope I had that he might change his mind at the last minute and agree to escort me to the Wentworths' party. Nevertheless, what hurt me the most was the implication that, while it was perfectly satisfactory for me to remain trapped at my aunt's all weekend, he was entitled to escape to the pleasures of Brighton, without even considering that someone might question his decision.

Colonel Fitzwilliam took a a sip of wine and gently patted his lips with his napkin.

"So, dear Georgiana, how was Lady Catherine feeling today when you went to see her?"

"She appeared weaker than usual, but in good enough spirits."

My cousin gave me a cautious look.

"I stopped to visit Dr Broughton on my way back from town. We have agreed that if her situation does not improve in the next few days, we will recommend her to return to Rosings as soon as she is able to travel."

The words were left unsaid, but we both knew the main consequence of Lady Catherine's leaving Grosvenor Square. With no formal chaperone to accompany me, no friends or acquaintances would do: I would have to go back to Pemberley.

My cousin was looking at me as if to check my reaction. I thought of my brother, Elizabeth, little Will and the baby that, God willing, would be born any minute. My heart swelled. I loved them so much. But as much as I adored the family home, it was no longer my own. My aunt had said as much. I had to find my place, and time was running out. It took all of my willpower to remain suitably composed.

"As you think best, Cousin."

His features softened, and he smiled. He was not a handsome man, but as Lady Catherine had said, he could be very charming. In the past, the Colonel had always been very kind to me, and had expressed his affection infinitely better than my brother; the Darcy reserve that I shared with Fitzwilliam didn't run on my cousin's side of the family. Nevertheless, the last few days had brought a change in his disposition towards me which had dramatically altered his behaviour, in a state of affairs I was not enjoying.

As if to exemplify this shift, Colonel Fitzwilliam took my hand to his lips, and this time he planted on it a moist kiss, a lover's kiss. I blushed violently.

"You are always so charming, dear Georgiana. The very essence of female modesty. You will be a great mistress of Rosings Park one day. The retired country life will no doubt suit you better than the foul London air."

I considered his words, remembering what my aunt had announced on the day of my arrival. I did have a home, after all. Rosings was a handsome building of relatively recent construction, with a great number of windows, in accordance with the new style for edifices of consequence, and no expense had been spared in furnishing the drawing rooms. It wasn't to my taste, but curtains, chimney breasts and wallpaper can always be changed. Still, I was unable to compare it favourably to my beloved Pemberley. My aunt's property was pleasant, but it was so different from Pemberley, so lacking in comparison that I could not think of it as home, or believe that one day I would see it as such. The noble landscape, the woody hills raw in their natural beauty, the lush grounds in the naturalistic style so painstakingly looked after by the Pemberley gardeners were to me infinitely more beautiful than the formal adornments so favoured by Lady Catherine.

However, I was alone in my relative indifference towards Rosings Park. My cousin's eyes lit up at the mention of my aunt's estate, and he seemed eager to discuss its many advantages. I dropped my gaze and stifled a yawn. Colonel Fitzwilliam caught my drift immediately, perhaps keen himself to finish our exchange.

"But I see you are tired, dear Cousin. Pray, retire for the evening if you so wish."

With that, he came over to my chair, offered me his arm, walked me to the bottom of the staircase, and if I had not insisted otherwise, I am sure he would have handed me to Jones herself. He watched me climb the stairs, his hand on the bannister like an adoring Romeo bidding goodnight to his Juliet.

Chapter 18

The following afternoon, when I arrived at Grosvenor Square after a walk in the park with Jones, I was astonished to see my brother's hat on a chair in the entrance hall. The footman came at once to inform me that he was in the second drawing room. With trembling hands, I removed my bonnet, gloves and shawl, and opened the door.

He was sitting in an armchair by the window reading the newspaper, a silver tray with tea things and some fruit cake neatly placed on a small table in front of him. As soon as he saw me, he stood up and came to greet me. My head was spinning.

"What news of Elizabeth?" I cried out, unable to swallow down my panic. "Why are you not with her? Has anything happened?"

He looked at me, his eyes tired but unusually animated, his

lips slowly drawing a hint of a smile, and I immediately knew she was well.

"Georgiana, I am delighted to inform you that you are the aunt to another bonny little boy. We have named him Charles. He was born four days ago, and both he and his mother are in good health."

Relief invaded my body, but the feeling was quickly replaced by another concern.

"And Will, is he well?"

"Very well. He is delighted with all the attention he has been getting. Everyone else is fine, as well, so you need not concern yourself."

My brother proceeded to update me on the Pemberley estate. Spring was in full bloom, the trees thick with leaves and flowers, the deer herd proud of their new calves, the fields alive with the bright green that comes with the good weather. His love of the family lands, even if for him they went hand in hand with duty, was second only to his affection for his family. The way he kept pressing the neatly folded newspaper in front of him, however, told me that something was troubling him. I wondered if it was the issue with the estate boundaries the Colonel had mentioned before I left Pemberley, but in the course of the conversation, Fitzwilliam confirmed it was on the verge of resolution.

My curiosity increased. If all was fine, if there was no news, good or bad, to report, and estate concerns, big or small, to resolve, why was my brother in London when his wife had just been delivered of an infant? Perhaps he had come to escort me back to Pemberley, although the Colonel was perfectly able to do so. I probed again.

"Colonel Fitzwilliam has been in touch about a most sensitive issue," he said after a brief silence. "He and our aunt seem to perfectly agree on an undertaking that concerns me greatly, and I wanted to discuss it with them at the earliest convenience. I was reluctant to come so soon after the birth, but Mrs Darcy insisted."

At the mention of his wife, my brother's features softened for an instant, but they quickly regained his usual seriousness.

"I was able to speak to Lady Catherine upon my arrival, but as you know, the Colonel is away until tomorrow. I suppose that he didn't expect me to come at all, or certainly not quite so soon."

He clenched his jaw, and his eyes avoided mine for a fleeting second. It was confirmation that the matter he was worried about somehow concerned me. However, he would not give me any more particulars on the matter and instead asked me about my time in London so far. I told him about the social engagements I had attended prior to Lady Catherine's illness and the new friends I had made along the way. I found myself mentioning Captain Wentworth and Mrs Wentworth a few times.

"Wentworth. Is that not the name on one of the invites arranged on the console table by the entrance?"

So he had seen it. Just as my aunt had instructed upon my arrival at Grosvenor Square, I had put the card right next to all of the other ones, on the carved console table in the hallway, which was the most visible spot for those calling. According to Lady Catherine, a carefully curated display of visitor cards and invites was the best way to communicate one's standing in society to any visitor to the house. Fitzwilliam must have seen the note from the Wentworths upon his arrival. I nodded.

"Captain Wentworth and Mrs Wentworth kindly invited Colonel Fitzwilliam and myself to dinner tonight, but at the request of the Colonel I had to decline."

I considered mentioning my dissatisfaction at his decision that I should not attend but the most pressing of social engagements, but I couldn't bring myself to censure the opinions of my other guardian. Fitzwilliam noticed my hesitation.

"Georgiana, your old brother knows you well enough to think that you would rather enjoy this particular engagement," he added, after some consideration.

I blushed.

"I would! Such pleasant company, and it is but a few streets from here. However, it is not to be."

I looked down to the floor. The design of the grand Turkish carpet that covered it was quickly dissolving into a blurry kaleidoscope of colours.

"Do you not think that the Wentworths might be amenable to accommodating a slight change of plans, even if it didn't include your original escort?" asked my brother in a gentle voice.

I glanced up. Fitzwilliam's eyes were smiling in my

direction.

"I'm afraid I do not understand."

"I would be delighted to make their acquaintance. It may be too late for tonight's dinner party, but we can issue our own invitation if you so wish. Unless your friendship with Mrs Wentworth is intimate enough to allow for such an irregular reversal of your original answer, that is."

My heart swelled.

"Oh, Fitzwilliam! Mrs Wentworth will be delighted to have us! If I say to them that you are in town you can be sure that meeting you will please them exceedingly."

"They must be worthy of the greatest respect and admiration if they have become such dear friends to you in such a short time."

I did not embrace him to express my gratitude because it had never been our way, but our exchange of affectionate looks and smiles was enough. I immediately sent for paper and quill, penned a short note for Mrs Wentworth and dispatched a messenger to Cavendish Square Gardens. She would be happy to have us amongst her guests; I had no doubt about it.

* * *

I had a very enjoyable lunch with my brother, who regaled me with little Will's most recent exploits. The cherubic and adventurous toddler, who was the spitting image of his father and had the vivaciousness of his mother, had become very fond of Mr Bennet.

"His grandfather captivates him with tales about engineering feats and historical events. They are an odd couple, but their affection is mutual. I suppose Mr Bennet never had the chance to instruct a son of his own, although Mrs Darcy must have been a perfectly adequate substitute at times."

We exchanged a knowing look. The desired male heir had never arrived for Mr Bennet, but he had enjoyed the company of an equally gifted, eloquent and witty mind under his roof in his second daughter.

After the meal, we retired to the drawing room, and the conversation took a rather disconcerting turn. After some minutes of silence, during which Fitzwilliam looked at me with an unreadable expression in his eyes, he took a deep breath and addressed me with a grave air.

"Georgiana, there is a delicate matter I would like to discuss with you. As you will be much aware, at your age it is generally accepted that a lady might start considering marriage. Lady Catherine has certainly made no secret of her expectations with regards to your London stay. Now, I know this somewhat forward of me, but have you become attached to a particular gentleman since your arrival?"

I was mortified. What did I have after three weeks in London but the realisation that my growing affection for Captain Price was a lost cause, both due to his lack of fortune and his imminent betrothal to Kitty Bennet?

"I wish Mrs Darcy were here to speak to you, but for obvious reasons it was impossible for her," said Fitzwilliam in an apologetic tone. "However, she was very firm in her instructions, and said in no uncertain terms that, if I am to help you guarantee your happiness, I have to find out from yourself directly whether your affections are engaged."

"It's hard to say, Brother," was all I dared to muster. "I have met many people in the last few days."

My brother, however, knew me too well. After giving me a few moments to recollect myself, he gently probed me again.

"Georgiana, I have been informed that your heart has been set on someone of our acquaintance for a long time now. Is that a fact?"

So he had been aware of my unrequited love for Wickham all this time. I wanted to tell Fitzwilliam about how I had finally seen through Wickham's dark soul upon meeting him at the concert hall and how his memory no longer had any hold on me, but I was dumbstruck. My thoughts, much faster than my lips, immediately moved to the Wickhams' sordid story of clandestine love and betrayal and the imminent duel with Don Cosimo. The details of the case were lurid enough to guarantee they would be poured over in every publication, and Wickham was sure to drag the Darcy family name down with his. A sense of panic started to rise from my stomach. My brother needed to know, but I was completely unable to mention Wickham's name out loud in the presence of someone who had been so wronged by him.

Who will tell him?

Fitzwilliam's hand was swiftly on mine. He was looking at

me with some alarm.

"You look pale, Georgiana. I am sorry I have caused you such distress, I will not say another word."

Just then, Fitzwilliam's eyes caught the jade clock on the commode, and his countenance changed. He immediately stood up.

"I am deeply sorry, Georgiana, but you will have to excuse me. I have a business appointment that I must absolutely keep. I will be back by five. Hopefully, you will have heard back from the Wentworths by then."

He was gone before I could utter a word.

Some minutes later, the footman came in with a quickly scribbled note from Cavendish Square Gardens. It confirmed that the Wentworths would be delighted to have Mr Darcy and Miss Darcy join them later that evening. I was very pleased with their answer, but my happiness was not complete. My thoughts had taken a dark turn, and there was but one thing I could do.

I rose from the sofa and sat at the desk by the window, in front of the remaining paper that had been brought in earlier. I had been unable to tell Fitzwilliam of the dangers looming over the family name, but he must be made aware of them. I must pen them down for him, and give him the note to read. I took the quill to the paper, but the words were unsatisfactory. I tried again, but it was no use. For the first time in my life, the written word was failing me.

I lost myself in the faint flicker remaining in the fireplace. There had to be a better way. As Georgiana Darcy, I was unable to give my brother the particulars of the case. However, what if the warning didn't come from me but from an anonymous friend? Caring to disguise my writing so as not give away my identity, I penned a short, unsigned letter informing my brother of the upcoming duel.

I had just finished folding the note when Cosette came in with word that Lady Catherine wanted to see me. I sent her back, saying I would be up at once. I slipped out of the drawing room, went towards the console table by the entrance and hid the letter for my brother in the pile of afternoon post. Then, I swiftly went up to the sick room.

* * *

Although Lady Catherine was still in bed, with a thick shawl over her nightgown, she was looking remarkably better. Her back was much straighter, barely touching the cushions placed to support her, and I guessed that Cosette had carefully applied a touch of cosmetics to give her a healthy appearance. I noticed that the little lapdog was napping on her lap, its small body tucked into a neat ball of black fur. I smiled inwardly; the poor thing would be pleased to be allowed back with its owner. My aunt was not in a good mood, however.

"Georgiana, I am most sorely disappointed. I hear that that you and your brother are going to the Wentworths tonight. What a waste of time. It would have been more convenient to leave things as they were. Even if your brother chooses to indulge you, it is rather selfish of you to insist on going against my and your cousin's advice. Darcy will be exhausted after the long ride from Pemberley."

For a moment I was ashamed, but then I remembered how Fitzwilliam had insisted on accompanying me. I reminded myself that I had his full support. I could feel Lady Catherine's cold grey eyes on mine, but I didn't look away.

"I don't understand this interest of yours in going to the Wentworths," she added with a grimace. "Unless it's because you're eager to see a particular gentleman, that is."

Her painted eyebrows and angular features gave her the air of an exotic mask, like the drawings of primitive wares I had seen in one of the books in the Pemberley library. I felt a shiver down my spine as if I was a helpless mouse about to be attacked by a hawk.

"If that Price sailor has taken your fancy, I have made my enquiries. He may be a favoured nephew of Lady Bertram's, but his family is lowly. His father is a drunkard, his mother is the hen to a brood of wild children, and they live on little more than charity from his uncle and aunt. Moreover, Captain Price has a lot less than he ought to, but it is not just because of the supposed events in his unlucky career which no doubt his friends will have made you aware of. His lack of fortune is also due to a rather unfortunate tendency of handing money out to hopeless causes."

I looked at her in the eye. I could not remain silent.

"Captain Price is a brave commander and a charitable soul. He was greatly wronged in the past and –"

"Insolent girl! You still harbour hope, I see, but it must be squashed once and for all. As my successor to Rosings Park, you will never marry so low beneath you, certainly not to an upstart who only wants your money. I will speak to your brother again, and he will soon come round to my way of thinking. Cosette, call for Mr Darcy at once!"

The maid came towards us with an anxious look in her eyes.

"I'm afraid Dewar said that Mr Darcy would be gone all afternoon, ma'am."

Lady Catherine let out a cry of frustration, and I felt I could breathe again. I was safe, at least for a few hours. But my aunt was not one to give up easily. Grabbing my wrist with her claw-like hand, she brought my face down to hers.

"You will marry as you are told, do you hear me?" she added in a whisper.

I shuddered.

* * *

Back in my room, Jones helped me prepare for the evening ahead. I picked my trusted *eau-de-nil* gown. It was not as richly made as others in my wardrobe, but I liked it very much and thought it ideal for a dinner among close friends. Jones brought me the butterfly brooch without asking, but I quickly pointed out that it wouldn't do.

"Of course, ma'am. The golden undertones will clash with the colours of your dress. How about your mother's diamonds?"

I thought of Captain Price's disdain for jewels and shook my head.

Jones nodded in silence as if she understood. She rummaged in my jewellery box some more, then took out the diamond cross that Elizabeth and my brother had given me for my eighteenth birthday. It was my favourite, but it had been banned by Lady Catherine during her initial inspection of my wares, and Jones had most obediently placed it in the barely discernible compartment hidden beneath the main section of the jewellery box.

I put it on. Its simplicity was perfect. I admired my reflection in the mirror and noted how the tiny stones caught the light and reflected it back. Through the looking glass, Jones looked at me and smiled.

At the agreed time I went downstairs. Fitzwilliam was waiting for me in the drawing room. With his dark green velvet jacket and starched breeches, he was the very picture of gentlemanly affluence and elegance. I searched his face for signs that he had read my anonymous letter or spoken to our aunt, to no avail. He seemed, however, very pleased to see me.

"You look beautiful tonight, Georgiana."

And suddenly I realised that I did.

Chapter 19

It was another mild evening, and it had been dry for a few days, so the streets were free from mud and dust. The conditions were perfect for a leisurely stroll, so Fitzwilliam said to the coachman that we would walk the half mile to the Wentworths, his sole duty to collect us after dinner. I took the arm my brother was offering, and we set off. The daytime bustle was waning, and in the dusk London had a magical air, the mist blurring the tall buildings in the distance and the skies above tinged in shades of pink.

Fitzwilliam looked pensive, and I wondered again whether he had read my unsigned warning, but I pushed the thought away; I had done all I could, and the rest was best left to the fates. After some minutes of silence, I could tell he was about to speak, and I braced myself for another uncomfortable discussion about my affections. However, to my surprise, Fitzwilliam asked me about the other guests likely to be at the Wentworths' party.

"I do not know for sure, but there will be a few Navy officers," I replied with some embarrassment.

"They are brave men, ready to risk their lives for this country. It's an endeavour that very few of us would dare to embrace, for which they are justly and handsomely rewarded."

"Not always."

I immediately felt my face redden. My brother gave me an inquisitive look, and before long I was delivering an impassioned account of the injustice suffered by Captain Price, proclaiming what a good, kind and honourable man he was. My brother listened attentively while I spoke, but I didn't dare raise my eyes to his as I did so, and we soon arrived at Cavendish Square Gardens.

The Wentworths' London residence was grander than I had imagined, an imposing three-storey house in white stucco with an elegant porch flanked by two Doric columns. Inside, our hosts gave us a warm welcome and expressed their unreserved delight at finally meeting Mr Darcy of Pemberley. Mrs Wentworth, in particular, was luminous, her evident happiness radiating around her with a gentle glow.

"I am so pleased to make your acquaintance, Mr Darcy," said Captain Wentworth to Fitzwilliam. "I will tell my brother Edward that I have had the honour to meet the man whose property he so praised all these years ago. He visited Pemberley during my time away and was rather struck by the place, so he wrote to me in one of his letters. True to his profession as a man of the cloth, he is a great believer in providence, and no doubt he will see divine intervention in our meeting. Now, allow me to introduce you to the rest of the party."

It was a small and very pleasant gathering. I feared my brother's natural reserve might come across as hauteur, but he was the perfect guest, asking the Captain for his opinion on the robustness of English ports in times of peace and praising the hostess for the comfort and elegance of their dwelling. He was, I realised, doing it for my sake because he knew how much I esteemed the Wentworths.

I thanked Mrs Wentworth profusely for allowing our belated acceptance of her kind invitation, but she waved my concerns away. She explained that she had initially invited Lady Dalrymple and Miss Carteret, as well as her father and sister. However, her cousins had declined on account of Miss Carteret's nerves being rather altered since the ball, and Sir Elliot and Miss Elliot excused themselves, citing a prior theatre engagement.

"So you see, Miss Darcy, you and your brother did us a favour by changing your mind at the last minute, or it would have been a poorly attended party indeed."

I protested; the size was perfect to allow agreeable intercourse with all guests, and at the same time it was large enough to facilitate new acquaintances and renew existing ones. Mrs Wentworth gave me one of her gentle smiles. Then, seeing that Fitzwilliam was busy consulting her husband about the most attractive spots in Shropshire for keen sportsmen, she looked at me knowingly, and I understood that the hip flask had been returned to its rightful owner. I felt my colour rise. Mrs Wentworth noticed my embarrassment and quickly steered our conversation towards gentler waters.

"I envy the easy camaraderie of men. Look at my husband and your brother; they were introduced but twenty minutes ago, and they are already in deep discussion. I must say, Miss Darcy, that your brother is as pleasant as I imagined him to be."

I smiled. Fitzwilliam was a worthy representative of the family he so prized.

A few minutes later, Captain Price arrived, and his gaze immediately alighted on me. His being commanded my attention like that of sunflowers in the presence of the sun, but I forced myself to fight it and remain calm. There were cries of welcome, and greetings, and introductions, and then he was in front of me. He had a kind smile and a twinkle in his eye, and I thought I had never seen him look so dashing.

"Miss Darcy, I was the happiest of men to hear from Mrs Wentworth that you would be here tonight. I was concerned about you."

I remembered the circumstances of the last time we parted, right after my unexpected encounter with Wickham. It felt like a lifetime ago. I smiled.

"Captain Price, please do not trouble yourself about my spirits. My distress that evening was more due to confusion than to affliction, although I'm afraid I must have appeared quite the feeble woman to you."

"Believe me, I know you to be the opposite."

His gaze was intense, and I had to look away, unable to bear the depth of my feelings. Attempting to change the subject, I gestured towards the Wentworths.

"The Captain and Mrs Wentworth appear very merry tonight."

"My lips are sealed on the matter, although I have no doubt that you will find out the particulars later."

He was openly smiling now, tiny creases forming around his blue eyes.

"I must say, Captain Price, you also seem very cheerful tonight. Is it on their account?"

"Miss Darcy, I am ashamed to admit that, as delighted I am for the Wentworths, I am even more elated at a change in my circumstances."

My chest tightened, and for a few seconds, I couldn't breathe. Were my fears to be realised? Was he to marry Kitty? I couldn't hear of it, not now. Without allowing him to add another word on the matter, I said with the utmost composure,

"What an extraordinary coincidence. My circumstances are also changing. I am to leave London shortly to return to Pemberley."

He looked at me with his eyes wide open. It was just an instant, but I saw them flash with panic. The bell rang, and all that I could do was to accept the arm he was offering me and enter the dining room with a racing mind and a heart pulling me in a thousand directions.

We weren't seated next to each other this time. My companions were Captain Wentworth and an elderly Admiral who spent most of the time dozing, and apparently had little inclination for social intercourse. His lack of conversation was more than made up by the Captain, who was exultant, although he wouldn't tell me the reason behind his joy.

"You must speak to Mrs Wentworth. She is looking forward to sharing our news with you tonight."

"Whatever it is, I am happy for you both, Captain."

He beamed back at me, a firm smile planted on his handsome face.

"Mrs Wentworth may have mentioned that we are leaving for Somersetshire in a few weeks. We are to spend some time with Admiral Croft and my sister. You must come and visit us at Kellynch."

"I thank you for the invite, Captain, I will miss you, although my London season is also coming to an end. I am going back to Derbyshire next week."

My companion looked at me as if it was the first time that evening.

"So it is true. My wife and I believe you to be a very remarkable young lady, and I speak for both of us in wishing you a very joyous life together." He must have sensed my confusion because he hastily added, "Marriage is not to be undertaken without serious consideration. You are still very young, but in my personal experience, age is not necessarily commensurate with wisdom in the matters of the heart. If you believe that your affections are constant and returned, do not allow the world to tell you otherwise."

His eyes were shining with an intensity I had never seen before.

"Oh, but I am not to get married, Captain–" I managed to whisper.

My head was spinning, and everything disappeared.

When I came to, my brother was looking at me with a frown on his face, pressing a glass of water to my lips, while Captain Wentworth watched with concern and his wife stood next to him, her face pale with worry. Captain Price was holding my wrist in his hand. A warm, manly, hardened hand, with short square nails grounded on perfect crescents.

"Miss Darcy only needs a bit of air, Mr Darcy. Allow me to accompany her to sit outside just for a few moments. I'm convinced she will recover in an instant."

His decisive air allowed no objections, not even from my brother. Holding on to the Captain's arm, I made my way towards the garden at the back of the Wentworths' house.

The warm night air enveloped me like a healing balm, and the fog in my head began to clear. The Captain made me sit on a bench overlooking the landscaped grounds, which were illuminated by the full moon, and he remained standing. I took in my surroundings. The garden was small, as was the case for most

London residences, but it was very prettily arranged, with a harmonic composition of shrubberies, fruit trees and flower beds. Above all, there were roses, in all shades of pink and as big as my fists, their sweet scent enveloping me.

I looked at the Captain, and for an instant, my affection for him was as tangible as the stone bench I was sitting on. I had never been so sure about anything in my life. And now he was to marry another. A weight took hold of my chest, and I gasped.

Noticing my distress, he lightly touched my arm with his hand.

"Take deep breaths; they will help you regain your strength."

I complied, and slowly recovered my spirits.

After a few moments, with great deliberation, the Captain joined me on the bench. He was a good foot away from me, but I could feel his presence as if he was a roaring fire in the coldest winter night. We sat in the darkness for a few moments, until he broke the silence to say,

"Miss Darcy, I am leaving for Portsmouth tomorrow and may not see you again for a long time. For this reason, I feel emboldened to ask you something. If I don't find out tonight, my heart will not only break but never recover, because not knowing is the worst of tortures."

His gaze was on me, frank and sincere. In the moonlight, his skin had the same grey undertone of the statues that decorated the garden around us, only he was flesh and bone.

"Captain Wentworth has said to me you are not to be married

to your cousin. May I ask if that is true?"

I pressed my hands together, shivers running down my spine, and I nodded. He gave a deep exhalation, then turned towards me with determination.

"Miss Darcy, I joined the Navy at thirteen, and I am a sailor at heart. I know not of the airs and graces of men of the world, and I am perfectly aware of my social standing at the moment, but please know that my words come from the heart, with no embellishment to disguise them. The first time I met you, at the roadside inn, it was as if I had known you all my life. You seemed to me the sweetest, most graceful creature on earth. Then I saw you again in London and realised just how superior your station was to mine. I must confess that I was bitter. It was just my luck that I should meet again a woman I could love, and immediately lose her to the conventions of society."

Love. He had said love. I started to tremble.

"I must confess I wished you poor because my fortune was far from large. I wished you blind, so you would not mind living in a modest house and see plaster instead of silk panels and fine wallpaper on the walls. I was in despair. But that has all changed. I have just received a letter from the Navy calling me to Portsmouth. I have been recognised for a capture I commanded under extraordinary circumstances, for which I did not receive any credit at the time, and I am due a large reward. My fortune is changing, madam, and the prospect of wealth has made me determined on my quest for your affections."

The contours of the garden greenery became a blur, and for a few moments, all I could think of was the scent of roses. Then, the Captain gently took my hand.

"Miss Darcy, I cannot in truth ask for your hand in marriage until the business at Portsmouth resolves itself in my favour. However, may I consider you my one and true love, the one I will marry one day?"

I looked at his kind blue eyes, the same ones that had captured my heart on the lucky day that our paths first crossed, and I nodded again, allowing the tears pouring down my cheeks to do the talking.

* * *

We didn't have much time together after that. I knew my brother would be worried, so we made our way back to the house, after having agreed to keep our promise of love a secret until after Captain Price's affairs had been put in order and he could formally ask for my hand in marriage as a wealthy man. The joy in my heart was overpowering. I had not entered a formal engagement, but I trusted him and knew it would come. Above all, I was certain that I had the love of a good man.

Back in the dining room, my brother took in my glowing cheeks and happy countenance with visible relief. The rest of the meal was a sweet ordeal, for my eyes only wanted to see Captain Price's, but propriety insisted they shouldn't. An hour later, I retired with the ladies to the comfortably furnished drawing room. Mrs Wentworth searched out my company and gave me the happy news that a Wentworth baby was expected before Christmas. I expressed my happiness at her and her husband's obvious delight. I knew they would be the most wonderful of parents.

The gentlemen joined us some time later. Although my gaze immediately looked for Captain Price's, I couldn't help but notice that my brother and Captain Wentworth were deep in conversation. I suspected it was political matters, judging by their grave demeanour. It struck me that, although very different men, they shared an unwavering commitment to their values and responsibilities.

The evening slowly came to an end. One of the servants came in to let us know that Lady Catherine de Bourgh's coachman was waiting outside when Fitzwilliam took me aside.

"Georgiana, there is an urgent and rather unexpected affair I must attend to just now. It requires a brief absence, and I will not be short of company, for Captain Wentworth has very kindly offered to accompany me."

He had a look in his eyes that I recognised at once. It was the determined gaze he had when the eastern part of the Pemberley estate, which was on slightly lower ground than the main building, suffered a catastrophic loss, and he had to rush out to help the tenants in the dozen cottages that stood there. Then, Fitzwilliam gave me one of his half-smiles.

"I have asked Captain Price to escort you home. I hope you

will not mind."

I felt a wave of happiness invade me, and nodded.

"Sleep well, Georgiana. We have much to discuss tomorrow."

I was elated at the thought of having the Captain all to myself for a quarter of an hour, or William, as I may call him now. The name was noble and purposeful, gentle yet strong, and spending more time with its owner was my greatest wish. I smiled at my brother and swiftly boarded the barouche with my escort. My excitement was such that I did not consider the extent of my brother's words, nor the nature of the matter that had so abruptly required his attention.

Chapter 20

When I woke up on Sunday morning, I was still in a daze. The ride home with Captain Price was way too short, but it gave us the opportunity to repeat our promises of love, his hand gripping mine in the darkness of the carriage. In what seemed like mere moments we arrived at my aunt's Grosvenor Square residence, and I had to bid him goodbye.

In the morning light, my remembrance of the night's events bore the haze of dreams, and the little voice in my head began to whisper that the Captain's words had been but empty promises of love, because no actual betrothal had taken place. Were the Captain's affections real, added the voice, he would have attempted to kiss me instead of being content simply holding my hand. However, I remembered his fervent words of devotion and his respect for my virtue and squashed the doubts immediately.

Captain Price was a man of honour, and he would be back for me, of that I was sure.

After getting dressed, I went downstairs with a mix of happiness and apprehension rising in my stomach. I did not know how I was to face Fitzwilliam without admitting my affection for Captain Price and confessing his resolution to marry me. The breakfast room was empty, and I quickly noticed that in my usual seat, leaning against a cup, there was a letter addressed to me. I recognised the handwriting immediately: it was Elizabeth's. I opened it with haste and read:

Dearest Georgiana,

Your brother will have informed you of the matters relating to my health and the baby's, so I will address the object of my missive with no further delay.

We have just received an extraordinary announcement from Grosvenor Square, a revelation that has come as a surprise to both your brother and myself. Its paramount importance and our concern for you are behind Darcy's visit and my letter. We must be certain that the course of action you are about to embark on is of your judicious choosing, and not a passing fancy or the result of undue influence deriving from other parties.

Marriage is to last one's lifetime, and whether we endure it or enjoy it depends to a significant extent on our doing. I remember the confusing emotions that meeting your brother stirred inside of me. Perhaps you are as aware of your affections as he was at the time, in which case my words will make little sense to you, but if you feel the faintest uncertainty, please read on.

Georgiana, I love you as much as my blood sisters, and I want you to be as fortunate in marriage as I am. I do not wish you the blandness that comes with tolerable companionship, but a union overfilled with devotion and joy. However, on some occasions, our luck is our own doing, and rather than stand still and hope for the best, sometimes we have to strive for it.

I pray that you may find the fortitude to discern sisterly affection from the love between husband and wife. If what you desire is what the Colonel has intimated, then, by all means, marry him. You will have our blessings and best wishes for happiness in your future together. However, if you have the slightest hesitation, I urge you to reflect on your feelings and act accordingly.

Although I am away from you, dear Georgiana, my thoughts are with you every moment, and I look forward to the day we will be reunited.

Your dearest sister,

Elizabeth

PS We cannot change our past, but we may learn from it and use its lessons to guide us in our quest for happiness.

I sat down, clutching the letter in my hand. The maid came, and I sent her away for some tea, although I had quite lost my appetite. I needed some time to reflect on Elizabeth's words on marriage, love and happiness.

In my eyes, the content of Elizabeth's letter highlighted the superiority of Captain Price, not just regarding the purity of his love for me, but also in the motives behind his affection. The Captain, I reflected, loved me for who I was. Had he not said that he had wished me poor? And ours was most definitely not a passing fancy, unlike Don Cosimo had been for me. I blushed at the recollection. The prince could never offer devotion and joy to a woman, but Captain Price was capable of that and much more.

My sister's letter also managed to convey in words the feelings I had for Colonel Fitzwilliam. Barring his bizarre behaviour of late, ours had always been a sincere and affectionate relationship. I had always respected him as a guardian and listened to his advice as a friend, but I could never see him as a romantic match. The reasons that were driving him to wish our marriage were unknown to me, although I suspected they were somehow related to my Rosings inheritance. At all events, his actions risked harming the confidence I had in him without achieving their purpose. My love for the Colonel was resolutely of the sort one may reserve for a favourite uncle, and could never be more.

I re-read the letter again, and this second time I was struck by the last line. Without mentioning him, I realised Elizabeth referred to Wickham, and I wondered what she thought of him. Wickham and Elizabeth had been acquainted for some time prior to her marriage to Fitzwilliam. Their ages were similar, and, although disparate in their character, they had similarly pleasant dispositions. What if there had been some sort of romantic attraction between the two? It would have been around the time Wickham was in the process of convincing me to elope with him. The prospect was too dreadful to contemplate.

The letter had unsettled me. I had the urge to speak to my brother, and I found him in the study. He welcomed me warmly and invited me to sit down. Still holding Elizabeth's letter in my hand, I looked at Fitzwilliam and noticed the blue circles under his eyes. How thoughtless of me. I had completely forgotten about his nighttime escapade.

"You look tired, Brother, but happy. I trust that the matter that came under your urgent consideration last night has been satisfactorily resolved."

Fitzwilliam nodded thoughtfully.

"Indeed, that's the case, I am happy to report. There is no closure as such, but all seems to be going in a more positive direction than I could have envisaged, and danger has been averted."

"Danger? What danger?"

He looked at me pointedly.

"I do not wish to alarm you, Georgiana, but had the events been different, the Darcy family name would have probably been tarnished by circumstances alien to us. I have to thank friends known and unknown for helping me prevent opprobrium for our kin."

So his sudden escapade had to do with Wickham. It had to

be. I thought of my anonymous letter and wondered if it had contributed to his awareness of the matter. I was aching to ask him what had happened, but my delicacy had prevented me from mentioning Wickham's name to my brother for years. Then, my gaze fell on a beautiful bouquet of roses above the mantelpiece. The scent that had so cloyed my senses the previous night overcame me, and with it, the realisation that my coyness was ridiculous. I was not a girl but a woman in love, and the past no longer had the power to haunt me.

"Brother, I need to know. Does that mean that Wickham did not kill his opponent?" I asked in a steady voice.

Fitzwilliam arched his eyebrows, but he quickly regained his composure.

"He did not. Captain Wentworth and Captain Price accompanied me to Primrose Hill, and the Italian prince was there, his silver pistols at the ready, but Wickham did not come. His friend Colonel Slater sent word that he was unwell. In fact, he is very sick, Georgiana. Years and years of licentiousness and dissolute living are catching up with him. I am sorry to inform you that he probably won't live long."

He wavered for a few instants, as if bracing himself for my tears, but I just smiled faintly. At first light on Primrose Hill, no blood had been shed for a silly woman and no news mentioning the Darcy name would appear in afternoon papers, which was all I wished for. Wickham's illness was secondary and came as no surprise; I had seen his decline for myself during my encounter with him in the concert hall. Wickham had wronged me, but I didn't see his fate as a deserved comeuppance. All I felt was a dull pity for a remorseless fool who had brought all evils upon himself with his debauched behaviour. I had nothing more to add on the matter.

On the other hand, the pink roses on the mantelpiece, silent but insistent, kept reminding me of what I had come to see my brother for. I took a deep breath and looked into the eyes of my brother.

"I have read Elizabeth's letter," I said in a steady voice. "Is it your belief that I intend to marry Colonel Fitzwilliam?"

"That is what we have been told. Is that not what you wish?"

I shook my head slowly.

"I love him, but I could never marry him."

Fitzwilliam assented, a sympathetic look on his face.

"He will be disappointed, Georgiana. Lady Catherine, too. They believed you reciprocated his feelings and thought the arrangement most convenient for the family."

"Dear Brother, in Lady Catherine's opinion such a match would be the best option for all parties, and I do not doubt her good intentions. However, although Colonel Fitzwilliam has a deep affection for me, like mine for him, it is not the same kind of love that a man should feel for his wife."

Fitzwilliam nodded.

"Georgiana, as your brother and tutor it is my responsibility to guide you through life," he added with a gentle voice. "As you well know, I promised our father on his deathbed that I would do my best to ensure your happiness. However, you must allow me to fulfil my vow by confiding in me."

In spite of his evident discomfort, my brother was insisting, solely for my sake. His eyes were sincere. I could not, I would not lie to him. Not again.

"You are right, Brother. I must admit that my feelings are engaged. I cannot say anymore for the moment, but please believe me when I say that nothing untoward has happened or will happen, and that you will be asked to give your assent in due course, after certain events have come to a resolution."

"Are those events by any chance due to take place in Portsmouth?"

Fitzwilliam must have seen the look of surprise on my face because he gave me one of his rare unguarded smiles.

"I should perhaps inform you that the gentleman in question has already made me aware of the situation, and, in view of his vehemence and the trust he commands in people I highly respect, I have given him my permission to pursue his object."

So he knew. He had spoken to Captain Price, and there were no dark secrets to hide from anyone anymore. I felt a wave of relief take over my whole body. Fitzwilliam came towards me, and put his hand on my arm.

"He's a good man, Georgiana, and I know you will be very happy. Now I must speak to Lady Catherine and tell her about your decision not to marry the Colonel. I suggest we keep any other news for now, until a formal announcement can be made next week."

Overcome by happiness, I whispered a thank you and saw him make towards my aunt's apartments upstairs.

* * *

Lady Catherine called for me shortly afterwards, and with a heavy heart, I went into her room. As always, she got straight to the point.

"What is this your brother is saying? Are you refusing your cousin? How can this be?"

"I do not think we are suited," I said with the most decisive tone I could muster. "We would not be happy."

"Nonsense! The Colonel is a perfect gentleman. I am sure you would reach an acceptable agreement. You have known him all your life, and are perfectly aware of his nature. Furthermore, what does happiness have to do with marriage?"

"Both my brother and his wife believe that it is essential."

"So because they fell in love everyone should be foolish enough to do the same? Look at your brother, one of the most eligible bachelors in England for years, the wealthy master of Pemberley with the looks and breeding of a prince. I would not have been surprised if he had escaped his destined union with Anne by marrying a baronet's daughter, a viscount's even. However, he squandered his standing and fortune in the world by marrying a social inferior for *love*."

She said the last word with disgust. I blushed. To have such little regard for everything that Elizabeth had brought to the family and to dismiss my brother's happiness as if he had acted on a schoolboy's whim! But there was no stopping her.

"I entreat you not to make the same mistake as Darcy. Do what anyone with common sense would and make a match with the Colonel. You are both related, and the families are known to each other. He has no fortune, but you have enough for the two of you. You shall be the Rosings heiress, he the youngest son of an Earl. There may even be a path to a title for you."

Her conjecture required two innocent little boys, her own grand-nephews, to die. Indignation began to burn inside of me.

"Of course, the Colonel is not a handsome man, but then again you are no beauty," Lady Catherine continued. "You would make a perfectly suited couple."

I couldn't help myself.

"Dear Aunt, I am well aware of my deficiencies, and that no matter how much I try to cultivate my talents and demeanour to appear more agreeable to you, my essential lack of outstanding physical beauty shall always act as a deterrent to your affection and respect. But pray, understand that there is no need to mention it every time we speak."

Lady Catherine was genuinely taken aback by my request, and for once did not open her mouth.

"I have already made it quite clear that I will not marry the

Colonel. I have my brother's backing, so please do not insist. Now, if you allow me, he is waiting for me downstairs."

I resolutely turned around and left the room, and as I closed the heavy door behind me, I allowed myself a triumphant smile. It perhaps looked like a trifle to others, but to me, that conversation with Lady Catherine was the most important battle I had ever fought and won.

* * *

The Colonel returned from Brighton late that night. I had already retired to my bedchamber, but I heard the door in the main entrance open and recognised his voice. I pictured his surprise and delight at seeing my brother, their cold supper in the study with a glass of whisky, as was their habit whenever the Colonel visited Pemberley, and I tried to imagine their conversation, but failed. The topic was delicate, and the stakes higher than they had ever been between the two cousins. Perhaps there was disappointment, possibly even a marked disagreement, but I never found out the particulars of their discussion. The only fact that Elizabeth let out in due course was that the Colonel confessed to having acquired substantial gambling debts since his return from Waterloo. His creditors had begun to hound him with letters, which had driven him to gambling more, and upon losing, to asking for more loans, in a vicious circle from which he saw no escape. In a desperate turn, he had decided that marrying me and becoming the master of

Rosings Park, which had always been his secret aspiration, was the only way he could afford to honourably pay his dues. His anxiety over the matter and the need to secure Lady Catherine's support had driven him to tell her about my sad affair with Wickham, of which he was deeply ashamed. He was, he said, determined to mend his ways and regain my confidence.

The following morning, Colonel Fitzwilliam was perfectly civil towards me, but his whiskers never again lingered on my hands as they had during the strange days before my brother's arrival, and he saved us both awkwardness and uncomfortable silences by leaving the following morning on a visit to his brother.

Lady Catherine locked herself in her chambers, and the servants were ordered to initiate the complex arrangements to close down Grosvenor Square for the remainder of the season that same morning. They covered the furniture with dusting sheets, shut the window panes against the inclement weather and the fading effect of the sun, packed all the trunks and carried them downstairs to be loaded on to the coaches due for Rosings and Pemberley, respectively.

While Jones took care of the packing, I fretted over Captain Price's return from Portsmouth. The hours of the day were slipping slowly, and I killed time walking in the gardens and talking to my brother, who was also visibly eager to get back home to his family. The fact that he had left them at such a time for my sake forever eroded any doubts that I might have on his affection for me. I also paid a short visit to the Wentworths, who were equally engaged with leaving preparations. Mrs Wentworth made me promise that we would write to each other and arrange to meet again in the future, and I was delighted to acquiesce.

Tuesday arrived, and with it, Captain Price. I was in the Grosvenor Square gardens when I saw him approach on his horse, his head held high, his countenance as determined as I had ever seen it. I rushed to the door, and caught him right before he went in. I was breathless, but before I could even regain my composure he smiled at me broadly, took my hand, ungloved it and brought it to his lips. I felt his kiss for the first time, soft and tender, and it sent shivers down my spine.

"It is done," he whispered in my ear. "I am a rich man, Georgiana. I must see your brother at once."

He was in the study with Fitzwilliam for less than ten minutes. When both men came out, they were in good spirits, and met me with alacrity, Captain Price to kiss my hand again and claim me as his beloved for the world to see, and my brother to congratulate me. The Captain appeared to be the happiest man alive, Fitzwilliam had the look of a man who knows he has done his duty, and I was certain to be blessed with good fortune in a way I had never dared imagine.

Epilogue

My brother was eager to get back to Pemberley as soon as it was practically possible, and we settled for Thursday at dawn. I still had not spoken to Lady Catherine since our spat, and although I tried, I never saw her again before leaving London. The servants, loyal to their mistress, were polite but firm, and insisted that she had given specific instructions that she should not be disturbed by me at any time. My brother, after a private conference with Dewar, managed to be received by our aunt, but it cannot have been a happy interview, for Fitzwilliam never mentioned its contents to me. I am ashamed to admit that my biggest regret was that I did not have the chance to say farewell to Lady Catherine's little black dog, which had stolen my heart.

The afternoon before our departure Jones came back from her last shopping expedition in London with the most astonishing news. It was all over town that Don Cosimo and Miss Carteret were engaged to be married, with the reluctant blessing of the Dowager Viscountess Dalrymple. The extraordinary development caught me off-guard, but after some reflection, I came to see it as understandable, inevitable even. Besides a substantial dowry, as a Viscount's daughter Miss Carteret had the aristocratic connections that, according to Lady Hamilton's intelligence, Don Cosimo so craved. There was some bewilderment as to Miss Carteret's acceptance, given the prince's shameful treatment of her and his very public relationship with Mrs Wickham, but I understood. I had seen her eyes light up with utter devotion for the man she loved, in a response disturbingly similar to that of my fifteen-year-old self. It was by no means a bad match for either of them, although I felt sorry for the bride-to-be, for I did not think Don Cosimo would remain faithful to his marriage vows for very long.

Once Mrs Wickham heard that we were due to leave London, she also sent a letter to Grosvenor Square. In the missive, written in her usual feisty tone, Lydia justified the incident at Lady Dalrymple's and the subsequent duel as the legitimate rebuttal by a loving husband of an attack on his wife's honour. She ended the letter with an urgent plea for money to fund the expenses derived from Wickham's sickness, as well as new gowns for her. My brother knew that, with their lack of a regular income and scarce notion of household finances, destitution would quickly come to the Wickhams, and his sense of responsibility towards his sister-in-law overrode any past qualms about her husband. Fitzwilliam arranged for them to move to a small cottage on the south coast; it was a simple dwelling, away from the temptations of society, with a single servant to tend to them. The arrangement was such as to give the Wickhams privacy and tranquility, with the secret hope that the husband might reflect upon his past behaviour and repent before his impending passing, and the wife might reconsider her ways. Whether my brother's goal was achieved or not, we may never know.

For me, returning to Pemberley was a true homecoming; I seemed to recognise every tree, every shrub, every bird, and the estate more beautiful than ever. In my happiness, even the Bennets and their squabbles at the dinner table seemed pleasant. Seeing Elizabeth again was a balm for my excited senses, and telling her everything that had happened to me helped me reflect on the many blessings I had received in just a few short weeks. My brother, for his part, was equally satisfied to be back with his young family, and appeared as besotted with his second son as he was with his first. Will initially watched the new baby with a mix of inquisitive suspicion and irrepressible affection, but knowing his kind nature, I had no doubt that the latter would prevail.

My last summer in my childhood home was unforgettable. Dr Robertson's forced absence from Lambton due to a professional matter may or may not be related to what happened, but with no bloodletting sessions, Elizabeth recovered surprisingly quickly after her lie-in. With her health came Mr and Mrs Bennet and Mrs Bingley's departure. Elizabeth's parents found it difficult to leave their daughter and grandchildren, but her eldest sister was clearly eager to return home to her husband, although she gave us her assurances that she and her husband would visit Pemberley again before Christmas.

I enjoyed a few weeks of perfect domestic contentment with my brother, sister and nephews, which only increased with the awaited arrival of Captain Price by Midsummer. We were married shortly afterwards, surrounded by family and friends, and remained at Pemberley for a few more months, during which the Captain became an indispensable presence in the Darcy circle. He was a trusted confidant to my brother, a charming conversationalist to my sister-in-law, and a fun playmate for my nephew, helping to mitigate Will's despondency at the departure of his beloved grandfather. As for me, what Captain Price represented, how my heart swelled every time our eyes met, the reader may imagine.

It wasn't until after the summer that Lady Catherine informed me via a visit from Mr Collins that she had decided to leave the bulk of the Rosings estate to Colonel Fitzwilliam. I was glad for the Colonel, for I trusted that he would use his wealth wisely and move on from the disgraceful state his finances were in due to his previous lapses into gambling. At the same time, my feelings surprised me. My aunt's decision was not a disinheritance as such, as her London promises had never materialised, but I did not find it half as unpleasant as one might think. William says that it is because deep inside I always knew that Rosings was not the place for me. Instead, when it came time to decide on where to settle, we chose a beautiful property by the sea, only half a day's coach journey from Pemberley, with a spacious and comfortable house that met our requirements perfectly in spite of not featuring a single fireplace worth more than a few pounds. The three little orphans that Captain Price rescued from misery and their mother live in one of the tenants' cottages, about a mile from the main building. The youngest one may never see properly, but his eyesight is better than it was, and this gives us hope.

We are happy, reader, very happy, and I feel like I'm the luckiest woman on earth. After Elizabeth, that is.

THE END

Acknowledgments

I would like to thank my close friends and family for encouraging me to put years of daydreaming into words and supporting my efforts on a practical level. I am also very grateful to my wonderful editor and very efficient proofreader, Helena Hamilton, for her advice and suggestions. Finally, I am much obliged to the wider Janeite community for receiving my contribution to the genre with open arms.

About the Author

Eliza Shearer is a long-time an admirer of Jane Austen's work and emerging writer of Regency romance and austenite variations. She can often be found enjoying long walks and muddying her petticoats, or re-reading Jane Austen's novels by the fireside. She is very partial to bread and butter pudding, but has never cared much for cards.

Miss Darcy's Beaux is Eliza Shearer's first book and the first one in her *Austeniana* series. To be kept up to date with her upcoming work please follow her on Twitter @Eliza_Shearer_ or visit https://elizashearerblog.wordpress.com.

22550386R00157

Printed in Poland
by Amazon Fulfillment
Poland Sp. z o.o., Wrocław